Dope

**Lock Down**

P.O. Box 944

Stockbridge, Ga 30281

**Visit our site at**

www.lockdownpublications.com

Copyright 2020 by Destiny Skai

Dope Girl Magic 2

**Lock Down Publications**

**Like our page on Facebook: Lock Down Publications @**

www.facebook.com/lockdownpublications.ldp

Cover design and layout by: **Dynasty Cover Me**

Book interior design by: **Shawn Walker**

Edited by: **Kiera Northington**

3

Destiny Skai

**Stay Connected with Us!**

Text **LOCKDOWN** to 22828 to stay up-to-date with new releases, sneak peaks, contests and more…
Thank you!

## Submission Guideline.

Submit the first three chapters of your completed manuscript to ldpsubmissions@gmail.com, subject line: Your book's title. The manuscript must be in a .doc file and sent as an attachment. Document should be in Times New Roman, double spaced and in size 12 font. Also, provide your synopsis and full contact information. If sending multiple submissions, they must each be in a separate email.

Have a story but no way to send it electronically? You can still submit to LDP/Ca$h Presents. Send in the first three chapters, written or typed, of your completed manuscript to:

LDP: Submissions Dept
P.O. Box 944
Stockbridge, Ga 30281

*DO NOT send original manuscript. Must be a duplicate.*

Provide your synopsis and a cover letter containing your full contact information.

Thanks for considering LDP and Ca$h Presents.

# Chapter 1

Tori finally pulled up to Eazy's house after being stopped by the redneck cop. Honcho was standing outside waiting on her. Expeditiously, he hopped into the car and she pulled off. "Where are they going?" she asked frantically.

"To the warehouses on SW 10th Street," he admitted.

"How do you know he's going to kill my dad? And what makes him think Diesel was behind Kilo's death?"

Honcho shrugged his shoulders. "Honestly, sis, I don't know. He wouldn't tell me. All I know is word finally came back that it was Diesel who put the hit out on Kilo." Honcho sat in the passenger seat and reflected on his memories with his only brother.

"I can't believe this shit."

"Why not? You knew Diesel didn't want you and Kilo together. It all makes sense." Honcho turned to look at Tori. "Don't you think so?"

Tori thought long and hard about her feelings towards Diesel. True enough, she hated his ways and him at the same time, the fact still remained he was her father. But Kilo was technically her husband. "Baby bro, all I can say is, I wouldn't put shit past Diesel. He has surprised me in more ways than one. But I would hate to think he would intentionally hurt me beyond repair by killing the love of my life."

Honcho and Tori remained silent until they hit SW 10th Street and turned off on the back street. When she hit the curb, Tori immediately spotted several police cars on the scene. Punching down on the gas, Tori sped up, doing sixty miles an hour until she was directly behind a police car. Slamming on brakes, she hopped out the car with Honcho on her trail and ran up to the crime scene. The sight of her father's truck made her have a fit. Tori was screaming and hollering as she tried to approach the truck, but the police grabbed her.

"Let me go. That's my daddy," she cried. Honcho grabbed her from behind and tried to restrain her. "Daddy! Daddy! Nooo!" she screamed and fought, trying to get loose.

Effortlessly, the muscle-bound cop was able to handle her light weight. Holding her by the shoulders, he gently pushed her against his car. He felt compelled to explain the situation to her, because he too, had a daughter at home. Therefore, he had compassion during her time of grief.

"Ma'am, please listen to me. I need for you to try and calm down and take a deep breath. We have not identified any of the victims just yet. Once crime scene has collected their evidence, you will be able to come down to the coroner's office and identify his body. What's his name?"

"Torin Price."

Tori just stood there in a daze with tears running a river down her melanin skin, while eyeing the bloody sheets that covered each body. The loss of two parents had begun to wear down on her weak frame. In slow motion, her body slid towards the ground as she lost the feeling in her legs. All she could think about was losing another important person in her life. Despite the hatred she displayed towards him, Tori still loved her dad.

Honcho kneeled beside Tori and grabbed her arms. "Come on, Tori. Let me take you back to the car."

"I'm not leaving," she sobbed loudly.

"I know. We're going to stay until we can identify his body. Just come on. I got you, sis."

Honcho felt bad for the pain his father had just caused Tori. He loved her like a sister, but at the same time, he understood why his father did it.

Three hours later, they were finally at the coroner's office. Honcho held Tori at the waist and escorted her to the back room. The spirit of death in the air rocked her soul. She could hear her heart beating through her eardrums. Once again, Tori felt a disconnection from life. All she knew was heartache and frankly the young woman was tired. It was like she was grieving her mom and Kilo all over again.

The closer they got to the glass, the more her body quivered. Tori found herself clutching onto Honcho a little tighter. The old man dressed in the white lab coat nodded his head in their direction and proceeded to pull the sheet from over the body. In that moment, Tori's heart dropped to the pit of her stomach.

***

"This muthafucka killed half of my damn men," Diesel shouted, while pacing back and forth on the back patio. All he could think of was the phone call he received from Eazy. "His bitch ass set me up."

"I told you not to trust that nigga." Byrd removed his black hat and sat it on the table. "I knew that shit was gone be an ambush."

Diesel ran his hand over his face and picked up the bottle of Jack Daniels. His Adam's apple moved rapidly as he chugged the hot liquor.

"Yeah, I know. That's why I took two trucks instead of one." He walked over and sat down on the metal chair. "Word must've got back to him that I had something to do with Kilo."

"That's 'cause you used them two sissy ass niggas." Byrd pulled out his pocketknife and flicked the blade open. Admiring the silent killer, he chuckled. "I told you to let me handle that shit. Them niggas ain't no real damn killers."

Regret was heavy on his chest and his friend of twenty plus years knew what he was feeling before he even said it. "That's what's fucking me up. I didn't want them to kill him. All I told them niggas to do was bring him to me. There was no need to pull the trigger because Tori already agreed to leave."

Byrd's eyebrow creased downward. "You sure about that, 'cause I know you couldn't stand that nigga."

"That's true." Rubbing his hands together, he looked over at the sparkling swimming pool. His voice was low and brittle. "Tori came here that morning to tell me she changed her mind. She said Kilo told her she should listen to me and leave." Diesel never felt guilty about taking a life, but having Kilo's blood on his hands was starting to weigh him down, like an anchor at the bottom of the ocean. The fact still remained that the boy was like a nephew to him.

"Let me ask you something." Byrd waited for Diesel to lock eyes with him. "Do you think Kilo really loved Tori?"

Diesel almost replied immediately, but he held his tongue. Then he thought about the question again and allowed it to register in his brain. Pushing his personal feelings to the side, he answered truthfully. "Honestly, I believe he did."

"And let me guess, you've felt that way all along?" His silence confirmed the answer Byrd was looking for. "Now you feel guilty because you took away the man she loved, all because of the hatred you have for Eazy."

Diesel cut his eyes at his partner. He already felt bad and he wasn't making the situation any better. "Bro, I get it. I fucked up. But guess what, that wasn't the first time I took someone away from her."

The sound of the back door slamming caused Byrd to grab his gun, without confirming who was present. But when he saw who was gracing them with their presence, he tucked his gun back inside the black leather holster.

Tori got one look at Diesel and rushed into his arms. The grip she had on him was tight. "Daddy, I thought you were dead. I didn't know what I was going to do without you."

Hearing those words melted his heart. "I'm okay, baby. A nigga gotta bring in the Coast Guard to take me off the streets."

Tori pulled away from his grip. "Who's trying to kill you?"

Instantly, he was caught off guard with her question, but he had to be quick on his feet. "They wasn't gunning for me. It's all good."

"Don't you think that's something I should know? What if my life is in danger?"

"It's not. My soldiers will take care of it." Diesel noticed the worry in her eyes. "I can provide you with a bodyguard."

"I don't need that. All I need to know is who's responsible so I can look out for myself. I don't need anyone playing under me."

"You'll be safe. I promise," Diesel assured her.

"I hope so."

"You will be. All you have to do is go and get your clothes and come back. I'll feel better knowing you under the same roof as me." Diesel shook his head the second she frowned. "Please, Tori. Do this for me. I'm begging you, baby."

"As long as your concubine is living here, I can't." Tori took a step back.

"That's the mother of my child. I can't just put her out."

"I didn't ask you to do that. I'm just saying I refuse to be under the same roof with her." She would rather drink bleach than to live in that house. "Look, I only came here to make sure you're okay. I have to go."

"Tori! Please don't leave." His pleas fell on deaf ears, as she walked back into the house.

# Chapter 2

So much was running through Tori's mind. She didn't know if she was coming or going. One thing she was certain of was getting to the bottom of the attack against her father. As Tori approached the porch, the door swung open. It was Eazy. He greeted her with a strong hug.

"It's so good to see you. I've been waiting for you to show up since you touched down, but I understand you've been busy."

"I've been making my way around." She let out a slight giggle.

"Come on, let's go inside so we can talk."

Tori followed Eazy into his study and sat down in the leather chair across from him. "So, what's going on?"

"First, I have something for you." Eazy opened the drawer and pulled out a bulky manila envelope. Sliding it across the table, he pushed it to the opposite of his desk. "Congratulations on your graduation. I'm so proud of you and I know Kilo would've been too."

Just the mention of his name still made her emotional. Tori wiped the lone tear from her eye. "Thank you."

Eazy leaned forward and folded his hands. "I need to come clean with you about something."

"Okay."

"A few weeks ago, I received some information about Kilo's killer. When I first caught wind of it, I wasn't sure if I should believe it or not. So, I did a little research of my own and confirmed the person was a reliable source."

"Who di—" Tori became choked up on her words. Taking a deep breath, she closed her eyes for a brief second before looking back into his eyes. "Who killed my husband?"

Eazy sighed and rubbed his head. "Your father."

"Wait, what?" Tori could not process the terrible news she'd just received. "No. No." Her hands began to tremble.

Eazy stood up and walked around to where she was sitting. He knew what her reaction would be, so he was prepared to comfort his daughter-in-law. Eazy held her hands. "It's a lot to digest. I know. This is how I felt when I found out the truth. The truth is, I didn't want it to be true. I knew Diesel and I would never make amends or come to some sort of truce, but I never thought he would take the life of my son, my firstborn. And for the past four years, I've been on the hunt to find out who was responsible for breaking my heart and yours."

Finally, she looked into his eyes. "Are you sure? Who told you this?"

Diesel took a deep breath and gave her every single detail about his discovery, including the person that snitched. The pain-stricken look on her face caused him to look away as he spoke.

*The warehouse was cold and silent, as Eazy and his goons sat anxiously for their guest to arrive. Ten minutes later, two of his soldiers walked in with a dude wearing a blindfold. They pushed him down in the chair and tied him up. Once he was restrained, they removed the bandana.*

*Eazy approached him with his hands behind his back. "Get to talking."*

*"About what?" Jarvis was nervous as hell.*

*"You know why you're here."*

*"No. I don't. I swear."*

*"Who killed my son? I heard it was you."*

*Jarvis began to panic and shake his head. "No, man. I swear it wasn't me."*

*"Well, tell me who pulled the trigger."*

*"Man, he gone kill me if I say something." Jarvis' eyes started to tear up.*

*Eazy snatched him up by the collar. "No. I'm gone kill you if you don't tell me who pulled that fuckin' trigger."*

*Jarvis was whining and slobbering out the mouth like the bitch they knew he was. Eazy pulled out a .45 caliber handgun and placed it underneath his chin. "Okay. Okay. Just don't kill me please," he begged for his life. "It was Sherrod, man."*

*"Who the fuck is Sherrod?" Eazy barked.*

*"This nigga from out the hood. I'll show you where he lives."*

*"Why did he do it?" The name didn't ring a bell to him, and Kilo never mentioned having any beef with a nigga named Sherrod.*

*Jarvis rocked back and forth in his seat, while shaking his head. He knew his days were numbered if Diesel ever found out he snitched. But at that point, he didn't have a choice.*

*"Diesel put a hit out on Kilo."*

*"Diesel?" Eazy stood upright and scratched his head. "You sure about that?"*

*"I'm positive, man. He wanted the man dead."*

*Eazy spun the gun, gripped the barrel and slammed it across Jarvis' head. "Arghh! I'm telling the truth. I swear. Don't kill me, please. I'm begging you. I got a baby on the way."*

*"I don't give a fuck. My son had a baby on the way too." Eazy tucked his gun away and reached into his pocket. In his hand, he wielded a Swiss army knife. He then leaned down and whispered in his ear. "I'm not going to kill you just yet. But I'm telling you right now, if you lying to me and I find out, I'm killing your whole family, Ms. Jackie too."*

*Jarvis' eyes stretched wide as a golf ball. He was shocked to hear him mention his grandmother's name. "I'm not lying."*

*Eazy grabbed Jarvis by the ear and used his right hand to position the knife beside his head. In two swift moves, he sliced off his right ear. Jarvis screamed and hollered at the top of his lungs.*

*"Get this bitch up so he can show us where to find Sherrod."*

Tori sobbed uncontrollably. "How could he do that to me? He knew how much I loved him. I hate him."

"You know I tried to kill him." Tori nodded her head. "You should also know I'm not going to stop until I do. I don't want any bad blood between us, because I love you as if you were my own daughter. I'm not asking for your permission. I'm telling you he's going to die. He took something from me and he must pay for it. I'll never harm you. Therefore, he has to pay with his own life. So, whatever arrangements you need to make, I suggest you look into it."

Tori didn't know what to expect when she came to talk to him, so she was sort of caught off guard. This time she grabbed his hand. "You love me, right?"

"You know that."

"You'll do anything for me?"

"Without a second thought."

"Okay, I need you to do one thing for me."

"What's that?" Eazy tilted his head to the side. He wasn't sure what was about to come out her mouth.

"Can you please give me time to get to the bottom of this? I want him to tell me the truth." His stare was blank, but his eyes were dark. Tori knew she was asking for a lot, but she didn't care. "In order for me to gain any peace about receiving justice for his death, I need him to admit it to me."

Eazy thought about it long and hard. In his mind all he could hear was *no*, but when he looked into Tori's eyes, he knew she needed answers if she was going to move on with her life. "For you, yes. I'll give you two weeks."

Tori dropped her head and exhaled with a sigh of relief. "Thank you."

"No problem." Eazy raised Tori's head with his hand. "Now, let me ask you a question. I never wanted to say anything because you were grieving, but I need to know."

"Know what?" she was confused.

"What happened to Kilo's baby?"

Tori was frozen like a deer in the headlights. She had no idea that Eazy knew about the pregnancy. No one knew. That meant Kilo told him as soon as he found out. Immediately, she felt pains in her chest for the decision she made four years ago.

"I had a miscarriage," she lied. There was no way she could tell him the truth.

"Damn, Tori, I'm sorry. I know you wanted nothing more than to have a part of him still running around after his death. I know I would've loved it."

"I'm sorry." Tori got up and ran out of the office and into the bathroom. To relive those final moments were unbearable. She regretted her decision every single day, but that was something she had to deal with for the rest of her life.

\*\*\*

Tori, Honcho and Dazzle sat at Lala's kitchen table taking shots of Belvedere, while playing spades. Throughout the game there was lots of laughter and trash talking going on. Quality time with her friends was the one thing she missed while in Atlanta. The only people missing was Kilo and Tweety. That was their entire gang. Now they were short by two. Whoever said time healed all wounds lied. Tori felt no better than she did on the day he died.

Each one of them tossed their final cards on the table. Tori scooped up the book since she won. "Y'all asses lost," she teased.

"That's 'cause you cheated." Honcho laughed.

"Nah, bro. You reneged trying to play footsies under the damn table." Tori giggled, while raking up the cards. "Listen, I need to talk to all of you."

"We all ears, what's up?" Lala asked.

"I'm about to open up shop again. It's time for me to get back into the game and this time, I'm taking over everything." Tori's phone rang. Jude's name popped up on the screen, but she silenced the call and went back to the matter at hand. "I'm going to meet up with my old plug and get some work. This time, I'm selling dope and weed."

"Oh, I want in on this shit." Honcho rubbed his hands together.

"No. I'm not about to be responsible for that. Then I have to answer to your daddy. Nope!"

"Girl, I'm grown. Stop playing with me. What the hell my daddy gone say? He always wanted me to join the family business with him and Kilo anyway, but I didn't want to."

"Okay, fine. You can move the weed. I know your classmates smoke a lot."

"Hell, yeah. I know all the spots up there. I can get this shit off in no time."

"Okay cool," Tori agreed.

"So, when we setting up?" Dazzle was excited about the news of stacking her own paper. "'Cause I need some coins."

"I'm meeting up with him in two days and I want all of you to accompany me to the meeting. He needs to see my team."

They all agreed to be in attendance.

"I need y'all to pull out your best attire for this meeting. This man has plenty of money and street cred, and you have to look the part."

"We got you." Honcho nodded his head.

"Thanks, 'cause I need all of you." Tori sighed in relief.

"Hey, Tori. Did you ever go by the house that night after the club?" Lala didn't want Honcho to know what they were talking about. However, Tori didn't catch on immediately.

"Huh?"

"That night we went out. You said you were going by to check on that house for me."

Tori thought a little while longer. That's when the robbery dawned on her. "Ohhh! Yeah. It was too late. I couldn't do anything, but we can discuss it later. I've had one too many drinks."

Time was ticking and it was getting late. Tori and Dazzle went their separate ways and left the lovebirds to be in peace. Tori called Jude back and linked up with him for the night. There was no sense in going back to her hotel just to be alone. She needed a warm body to cuddle up with.

# Chapter 3

Jarvis stood in the mirror, looking at his latest war wound. "I can't believe this crazy ass nigga cut of my fuckin' ear." He groaned from the pain. After the torture tactic, he ended up in the emergency room, getting it reattached.

On his way out the bathroom, he made his way through the small apartment and sat on the couch. Rubbing his hands through his hair, he took a deep breath. When he looked up, Lisa was standing in front of him with her hand on her small, round belly.

"Are you okay?" Her squeaky voice little voice matched her itty-bitty frame. Lisa looked no older than twelve, but in reality, she was seventeen and pregnant with her second baby.

"I'm good. Go back in the room. I don't need you in here talking my damn ears off. I just want to relax and watch TV," he stated with irritation in his voice.

Lisa sucked her teeth in return. She wasn't in the mood for his slick ass mouth or attitude. "Boy, please. How can I talk your ears off, when you only have one good one?" Lisa laughed loudly, while slapping her leg.

"That shit ain't funny." He picked up the remote from the glass table. "Ya' ass was in that hospital crying like a big ass baby."

"I know, baby. It was a joke."

Jarvis picked up his bottle of pain pills and dropped two into the palm of his hand. Tossing them to the back of his throat, he chased it down with a cup of gin. "Goddamn, that shit strong." Lisa stood there with her arms folded and rocking on her heels. "What, man?"

"Stop calling me man."

"What, Lisa?"

"I need some money."

"For what?"

"Why do I have to tell you what I need money for? That should be obvious, stupid. I don't have a job and you supposed to be taking care of me. I am carrying your baby, just in case you forgot."

"Man, you aggravating as fuck. And you wonder why a nigga take his time coming home." Jarvis dug inside his pocket and pulled out a knot of money. He peeled off three hundred dollars and tossed it onto the table.

Lisa didn't waste any time picking up the cash. "Throw it all you want to. I don't give a fuck. As long as you give it to me."

"Shut up, damn! You talk too fuckin' much." Jarvis knew how she was, and he continued to let her upset him purposely.

"So, the fuck, what. I wish you would've stayed away too. As a matter of fact, I wish I didn't get pregnant by your dumb ass. I let you get me kicked out my mama house, like a fuckin' dummy."

"Man, go in the room before I slap the shit out of you." Jarvis rose to his feet and pulled up his pants. He was ready to slap the taste out her mouth. But the knock on the door stopped him in his tracks. "You just got saved."

Jarvis opened the door to let his homeboy in. "What's up, boy?" Moon dapped him up, as he walked inside.

"Just coolin' and tryin' to relax, but I can't cause this muthafucka in here getting on a nigga nerves."

"Y'all wild. Wassup, Lisa?"

"Hey, Moon."

"You in here giving my nigga a hard time?" he joked.

"Nope." Lisa sat on the opposite side of the sofa where Jarvis was sitting and closed her legs. "He's just being moody, as usual."

"Lisa, go in the room," he quickly dismissed her, but she ignored him and continued to engage in a conversation with Moon.

Highly irritated and out of patience, Jarvis slid over and backhanded Lisa in the face. *Whap!*

The loud clap caught both Lisa and Moon off guard. "Yo, fam, don't hit your lady, man."

"Nah. She being disrespectful, fam. Take your ass in the room." Lisa grabbed the side of her face and darted in the direction of their bedroom.

Moon shook his head and pulled out a pack of Newports. He took one cigarette out and lit it. Then he tossed the pack to Jarvis. "Take one, nigga, 'cause you need it."

"I'm getting sick of her ass, for real. She keep pushing my buttons."

"She pregnant and emotional. Just ignore her ass." Moon took a pull from the cancer stick. "Just don't hit her, and not in front of me."

Jarvis lit his cigarette and took a pull. "Yeah, I hear you."

Yeah, a'ight. Anyway, what's the plan, now that you turned on Diesel and the nigga still breathing? You know we can't get no dope from him."

"Shidd, I got a little bit of money stashed away and some work left. I'm still gone hustle, but it won't be much."

"Yeah, you better lay low."

"I already know. By the time this war over, all them niggas might end up dead. Once that happens, then we on. We can take over this shit."

"And what about fine ass Tori? What you gone do about her?"

"Don't worry about Tori. My plan to get rid of her is already in motion."

"I see you been plotting." Moon chuckled.

"And you know this. I still owe that bitch for hitting me in the head with that gun at the store and for killing my lil homie. I'm gone show her this a man's game and that her position is on her back and not in the streets."

"Damn, you wanna rape the bitch?"

"Shidd, I just might. It depends on how I'm feeling when it goes down." Jarvis smirked, as he thought about getting revenge on his old boss. His dick got hard just thinking about it.

**\*\*\***

Tori arrived at the Ocean Manor Resort on the beach as instructed. Using the key to gain entrance, she stepped inside. Enamored by the view, she placed her hand over her heart like she was pledging to the flag and smiled. "This is beautiful."

"Not as beautiful as you." Jude complimented her daily.

On the marble tiled floor, there was a trail of red roses that led in different directions. One of them was to the massage table. The other was to the bedroom, she assumed. Jude inserted himself into her personal space and placed his hands on her hips. "I hope you like my surprise."

"I love it."

"Well, go ahead and shower. The lady went downstairs, she'll be right back."

"Okay."

"Put on the robe I left in the bathroom for you." Jude smacked her on the ass. "Go handle that."

Tori proceeded to the bathroom, stripped out of her clothes and stepped into the marble, walk-in shower. Since she had already taken a shower before she arrived, she took a bird bath to wash off the scented lotion and perfume on her skin. After the wash off, Tori draped herself into the white and gold robe hanging on the towel rack.

Jude was waiting beside a short, dark-skinned woman. She smiled and patted the table. "Come on over, remove your robe and hop on."

Tori did as she was told. Completely in the nude, she laid on the table. The woman covered her backside with a sheet and dropped some oil on her back. Closing her eyes, she allowed her body to relax, as she listened to the sound of the ocean. The softness of her hands caressing every inch of her upper back released the weight of the world she'd been carrying on her shoulders.

Rough, yet filled with pleasure, the masseuse squeezed her aching, tensed muscles. It was the best feeling on earth. Slowly, she moved down to her lower back, where her tramp stamp was located and went deep. Tori could instantly feel her spine tingle. She could get used to that type of treatment on a daily basis.

Tori closed her eyes and went into autopilot. Within the next few minutes, she was out like a light. One hour later, Tori was awakened by Jude. "Wake up, baby." He shook her gently.

Tori blinked a few times. "Huh?"

"It's over with, baby." He chuckled.

"Damn, already?"

"Yes. You can get another one later." Jude helped her up from the table and onto her feet. Then he draped the robe over her body.

Once the young woman was gone, the couple sat down for a candlelight dinner on the balcony. The sky was dim, yet the full moon lit up the universe with star dots. It was truly a beautiful sight to see. Jude served her a lobster tail, red garlic potatoes, a Caesar salad and a bottle of Moet to wash it down. As they enjoyed their meal, the two engaged in small talk.

"How are you feeling? I know you've been stressing lately, so I wanted to help you relax and take your mind off of things."

"I'm feeling much better, thanks to you. Let me find out you know what I need." Tori smirked while placing a potato in her mouth.

"I aim to please," he grinned, revealing his pearly white teeth. "A real man knows what his woman wants without her having to say it. With me, you will never have to tell me. I pay attention."

"Well, that's good, because I hate explaining things that are obvious."

Jude took in every hint she dropped into his mental Rolodex. His mission was to learn her, inside and out. Her strengths and her weaknesses. "So, how was your day?"

"It was pretty good. I spent most of the day looking for places."

"Did you find something?"

"Not yet," she sighed with a hint of disappointment. "I didn't like anything the realtor showed me, but I'll find something soon."

Jude cleared his throat. "You know you can live with me. I would love to go to sleep and wake up to your beautiful face every day."

While she was flattered and appreciated his gesture that was an invitation she had to decline. Yes, she liked him. She even enjoyed being with him daily, but that wasn't enough to make her shack up with him after a short period of time. "That sounds good, but I can't do that. It's too early and we're still getting to know each other. I don't want to rush into things. I still have my house, but I put it on the market."

Jude was disappointed, but he couldn't let her know that. "It's cool. I'm not trying to rush you. Just know the offer is still on the table in case you have a change of heart."

"Thank you. I'll keep that in mind."

"You don't have to thank me. That's my job as your man."

Although she never made it official, Jude always referred to her as his woman. *Maybe I should though*, she thought. He was definitely the type of man she needed in her life.

"My man, huh?"

"You heard me loud and clear."

"I did." She nodded her head. "I think I like the sound of that."

"You think or you know?"

"I know." She was infatuated with his thuggish demeanor.

"Tell me I'm your man."

Tori pushed her seat out and walked over to Jude. Straddling his lap, she placed her hands behind his head and planted soft, sensual kisses on his lips. "You're my man."

"I think we should take this to the bedroom."

"I second that," she giggled as he raised up, holding her in his arms. Jude carried her into the bedroom for a long night of lovemaking.

# Chapter 4

The meeting with Domino had finally arrived. Tori had been anticipating that day since she landed in the Sunshine State. Setting up shop and expanding was her only focus. Honcho, Lala and Dazzle were at her side and ready to ride. Tori adjusted her designer shades and swiveled her head towards the backseat, as they pulled in front of the house. "Y'all ready?"

"As ready as we gone be." Dazzle picked up her purse and sat it in her lap.

"I'm ready to get to the money," Lala stated.

Honcho parked the truck and silenced the engine. "Let's go."

Tori stepped out looking like a million dollars, rocking a royal blue pencil skirt, a seductive white blouse and a pair of gold stilettos to compliment her attire and a matching Chanel bag. Lala and Dazzle complimented her style in their designer business suits. Honcho clutched the duffle bag in his left hand and escorted the ladies to the door. His three-piece suit had him looking like he just stepped off the *GQ* magazine.

The door swung open and they were greeted by his bodyguard. He was big and buff, sporting a bald head, looking like Deebo. After letting them in, he stopped Honcho. "I need to pat you down first."

"Nah. I don't think so, homie."

His focus was on the bulge on Honcho's hip. "You strapped?"

"Is grits grocery?"

"You have to leave that at the door. Or I can't let you in."

Before Honcho could reply, Tori stepped in. "I'm sorry, but that's the only way I travel. Domino knows me, so can you tell him to come out here."

"What's the problem?" Domino appeared out of nowhere.

"My protector is packing and he wants him to disarm himself, but you know I'm here for business only. Just like before."

Domino stroked his chin, while checking Tori out head to toe. He admired her hustle and the way she conducted business. In his mind, she wasn't a threat, but he wasn't too sure about her gunman. Under any other circumstances he wouldn't have it, but for her he would let it slide. And that was only because he found her very attractive and felt it would benefit him in the long run.

"It's cool. Let 'em pass."

"Thank you." Tori kept her poker face on. She peeped the way he looked at her, so she needed him to know it was strictly business between them. Nothing more, nothing less.

In silence, they walked into his office. The bodyguard stood at the door with his arms folded. Honcho did the same, as he took his place beside Tori. Lala and Dazzle stood behind her. They too were strapped, just in case shit went left.

"I see you brought your crew."

"As I told you I would." Tori crossed her right leg over the left one. "Now can we get down to business?"

"Yes. Of course, but aren't you going to introduce me to your people?"

"My apologies. This is Honcho, Dazzle and Lala." They exchanged greetings and carried on with the task at hand.

Domino picked up a black duffle bag and placed it on the table. "That's fifty kilos as promised."

"Honcho." At the call of his name, he grabbed the work and sat the money on the desk. "Five hundred grand as promised. Feel free to count it."

Domino folded his hands and placed his elbows on the oak wood desk. "No need. I'm taking your word, just like you're taking mine. This is where we establish trust. If anything is missing, I'll see you when you come back. If you don't return, I'll find you."

"Understood. But you sure you wanna do that? I don't need no issues when I come back."

Domino stood to his feet and grabbed the bag. Using his forearm, he treated it like a set of weights by raising it up and down to get a feel of the weight. "I know it's there. I've been in this game a long time, sweetheart."

"Suit yourself."

"It was nice doing business with you." Domino extended his hand.

Tori rose up and met his stare, while shaking his hand. "Likewise. I look forward to doing business with you for an extended amount of time this go-round."

"I hope so." Domino placed a kiss on her hand. It made her uncomfortable, so she pulled away slowly. She didn't want to offend him, but he needed to know where they stood. "I'll be in touch when the weed arrives. I'm expecting some good Crip in a few days."

"I'll be ready."

"A female hustler. My kind of woman." He grinned.

"That's all I know." Tori winked and did an about-face. It was time to hit the block running.

***

### Oakland Park Trap House

Surrounded by a group of young, hungry hustlers, Tori sat at the head of the table like she was the cocaine godmother. It wasn't reality just yet, but it was her ultimate goal. With the right soldiers on her team, it was possible. *If only Kilo was here, things would be so much easier,* she thought. Tori couldn't wait to get rid of the house she was standing in.

No matter how hard she tried, Tori could never shake those thoughts. Kilo was constantly on her mind and in her heart. The torture was in his absence, knowing she'd never see him again in life and there was nothing she could do about it.

Snapping back to reality, Tori looked into the eyes of her crew. She had all the power needed to become a certified boss, with a group of soldiers that looked up to her. Everyone in attendance knew all about her father and they feared him. But they also knew she could hold her own and wouldn't hesitate to pull that trigger. Her late husband taught her that. The newest members knew about the body she dropped at her kitchen, but they lived by the code of the streets. Therefore, that news never left the hood. Nor did it make its way to the police station.

"First, allow me to thank everyone for showing up and being on time. That's a major pet peeve of mine and I can promise you, you don't want to see my dark side. My time is valuable and I need every last one of you to treat it as such." Tori scanned everyone's faces to make sure they understood where she was coming from. Their head nods suggested that wouldn't be a problem.

"Everyone in here has their own clientele and hustling spots, so not much is going to change. Except the fact that there are some hot spots I want to invade slowly. Tank, Ace and Max, since y'all pretty much run the Fort Lauderdale area, I want y'all to recruit your own individual foot soldiers and expand from Sunland Park to the beach. I want everyone copping work from us. Honcho, you'll be working alongside me, as well as pushing the weed in Atlanta. Fresh, I don't have to tell you what to do because you already know."

"Oh, Milo come home next week, so he'll be on board when he touch down," Fresh added.

"Cool. Just bring him to see me. Last, but certainly not least. Dazzle and Lala, y'all will make deliveries to our distributors and help me break down the work when it arrives. We only have a few right now, but that will pick up soon. You two are to deliver together at all times."

"Okay," they responded in unison.

"Now, I will tell you Diesel has a few of his soldiers running in and out those spots, but my goal is to get them out the way. So, don't let that deter you, just in case you run into them."

"Them niggas gone get down or lay down. Simple as that," Max stated, while slapping fives with Ace. Max was the rebel in the group. Ace was more laid back. The silent type who'll kill you quietly like high blood pressure.

"I'm ready to light some shit up." Tank grinned. He was known for carrying heavy artillery.

"That's what I need to hear, but we need to use enforcement when necessary. If you can bring them on without a battle, then that's better. The goal is to make money and with a war going on we can't eat, so let's be smart about it."

"I agree." Fresh eyed the younger hustlers. "So, y'all keep a cool head out there and if you need help call me. We don't need no crash dummies on the streets. I'm trying to stack my money."

"Understood fam," Tank replied. Ace and Max simply nodded their heads.

"Don't hesitate to call me either. We're all family here and we have to look out for each other. I'm not tolerating any beefing amongst us. We all gone eat, so there won't be any reason to hate on the next. And most importantly, no snitching. We don't do that shit around here. I don't care how bad it seems, I'll find a way to get you out, but you need to have patience and stand ten toes down." Fresh knew the game from the depth of his soul. Greed could ruin Tori's organization, so he made sure to have her back and rule with an iron fist.

There were multiple mumbles throughout the room about not being snitches. Satisfied with her meeting, she ended it. "Well, if no one has any concerns or questions, you're free to go. Grab your bags on the way out. When it's time for the re-up, bring them with you." Seconds later, the room was clear with the exception of Honcho.

Watching her closely, he felt like something was wrong. "You good, sis? Something on your mind?"

"I'm good. I'm just ready to get rid of this house, that's all." Tori took a deep breath and exhaled slowly. "It's too many memories of Kilo in here. Every time I pull up in this driveway, I can see him lying on the ground bleeding, and that disturbs my soul."

"What the realtor talking about?" Honcho leaned against the counter.

"She has someone coming here tomorrow to look at it. That's why I held the meeting here. But now that we have people interested in the property, I'm not holding any more meetings here."

"It's gone sell, just chill. I mean, you living at the house with Pops, so you good. He wants you there anyway so he can watch you like a hawk," he chuckled.

Tori giggled. "Nah. He been telling me to move on for the longest."

"You should. It's been four years. It's time."

"Well, I met someone. We've been talking. I like him, but it's nothing serious. I'm just taking my time, you know."

"Yeah, I get it." He too agreed Tori should move on. "On another note though, you need to look into purchasing a duplex so these boys can trap out of it. And depending on how many units it is, you can rent out the others."

"That's a good idea. I do need to have verifiable income. I was thinking about opening up a hair store too."

"Invest that money. Shit, I ain't gotta tell you what to do. You went to school for accounting."

"You right about that. I'm working on it though." Tori looked down at her watch. "I need to go to Wells Fargo bank before we go back to the house."

"Let's ride then."

Upon their arrival, Honcho pulled up near the front entrance and let her out. Tori walked inside and filled out a deposit slip for two thousand dollars. There were two people in front of her, so the wait wasn't long at all. Approaching the counter, the teller smiled.

"Good afternoon. How are you?"

"Hello. I'm good. How is your day?" Tori slid the slip and the cash to her.

"Ready for five o'clock to hit, that's all."

"I can understand that."

The teller looked at the slip. "May I have your license please?"

"Sure." Tori retrieved her wallet and passed over her license.

The young woman checked the ID against the account and looked up at her face. "I'm showing a different name on this account. Did you give me the correct number?"

"Yes. It's not my account. I'm depositing the money into someone else's account."

"Oh okay. No problem." Once the transaction was complete, the teller handed over the receipt. "Have a good day."

"You as well." Tori walked out the bank feeling accomplished, but guilty at the same time.

# Chapter 5

### Later on, that night

Mya had a long day at school and her night job at McDonald's. No one told her being a teenage mother would maybe such hard work. Especially without the help of her child's father. However, she appreciated Tweety for stepping up and helping with the baby since Tron was locked up. The girl was truly a blessing.

It was just after eleven and she couldn't wait until she made it home. All she wanted to do was shower and go to sleep, so she could get up at six and start her day all over again.

Mya walked down Atlantic Boulevard in Pompano, with her earbuds in her ear. Thankfully, the apartments she lived in with her mother was literally up the street, so it only took fifteen minutes for her to arrive by foot. Loudly, she sang, "Have You Ever" by Brandy.

"Have you finally found the one you've given your heart? Only to find that one won't give their heart to you. Have you ever closed your eyes and dreamed that they were there and all you can do is wait for the day when they will care?"

Mya had the voice of an angel and she never hesitated to sing in public. Tears rolled down her cheeks as she sang her heart out and thought about Tron. She loved him, but she didn't feel like he loved her in return. He was far too gone with Tweety.

Looking across the three-lane highway, she waited until the road was clear before crossing the street. It was dark as hell outside, but the street was well lit and she had her can of mace in her pocket. They didn't live in the ghetto, but she was definitely in the hood.

Mya walked through the gate and went into her building. There were a few boys outside, but she ignored them. Old memories of her and Tron crossed her mind, as she strolled past Dazzle's old apartment. That was where their son was conceived.

As she walked into her apartment, the stench of a burning crack pipe invaded her nostrils. The smell made her stomach hurt. Mya couldn't wait to move out. She had it up through the roof with her mother and the freeloader she swore was her man. Mya couldn't understand why he was there. Baldhead worked side jobs, but Mya didn't see the benefit, since her mother still begged her for money. Mya knew he was high because he was stuck staring at the ceiling and his sleeves were raised, revealing track marks.

"Did you bring me some cigarettes?" Cynthia looked up long enough to beg before she put the pipe back to her lips.

Mya rolled her eyes and frowned in disgust. "No."

Cynthia's appearance was beyond disgusting. Her hair was mangled and stood up on her head. The tee shirt she wore was dingy and her titties sagged since she wasn't wearing a bra. Upset that her daughter didn't listen, she rose to her feet shouting. "I told your ass to bring me some fucking cigarettes."

Mya was tired of the begging. She had to care for herself and her baby. There was no way she was supporting her mother's habits. "You have a whole man living here. Why can't he buy your cigarettes? I have a child to take care of and I have to take care of myself. You don't help me, remember?"

"You live here, so yeah, I do take care of you."

"Whatever." Mya waved her hand, brushing her off and went onto the kitchen.

Cynthia was still talking shit. "You don't take care of that baby. Tron girlfriend do. So, I don't know who you think you fooling. I know one thing, yo' ass gone start paying rent."

Mya fixed her a cup of water and tried to exit the kitchen, but her mother was blocking her way. "Can you move? I'm tired. I have school in the morning and work in the afternoon."

"That ain't my problem. Nobody told your fast ass to be fucking a grown ass man and get pregnant." Cynthia scratched the area between her breasts.

"Well, if my mama wasn't too busy on a glass dick and gave me some guidance, I wouldn't be in this predicament."

Cynthia lost all control of her hands and slapped Mya across the face. "You better watch your mouth, you little bitch. I brought you in this world and I'll take your ass out."

Mya's face stung for a second, but she shook it off and her reflexes kicked in. Raising her hand, she slapped her mother back in the face.

Cynthia grabbed Mya by the hair and dragged her into the living room.

"Bitch, I'mma show you who not to play with."

Cynthia forgot it was her daughter she was fighting and threw back to back punches in her face. Mya blocked some and landed a few punches to her mother's face as well. There was an all-out brawl going down and Baldhead was still in his own world.

Mya tried to pull herself from her mother's grip, but crackheads had superpowers when they were high.

"Let my hair go, bitch," Mya screamed at the top of her lungs, while plunging her fingers into her mother's eyes.

The fight continued for several more minutes until they were interrupted by loud banging on the door. "Police! Open up!"

Cynthia released Mya's hair and tried to fix herself up, but there was nothing she could do to make herself look any better. Rushing to the table, she grabbed the crack pipe and put it under the sofa cushion and wiped her mouth with her dingy shirt. When she opened the door, there were two cops standing there with curious eyes. One was black and one was white.

"We got a call about a disturbance." The white cop used his right hand to push the door open. "Who's in here with you?"

"Um." She tried to smooth down the hair on her head. "My daughter. We just had a little disagreement."

"I need to verify that." He pushed his way inside to get a closer look, with his partner in tow. Mya was standing there battered and bruised.

"Are you okay?" he asked.

Mya shook her head. "No. I'm being abused."

"How old are you, ma'am?" the black officer asked.

"Seventeen." She was a few months shy of her eighteenth birthday.

The officers looked at each other. "What do you want to do? Do you want to take the mother in?"

The white officer placed his hand on his billy club. "I don't think that will work. We take her in tonight and she'll be let out on her own recognizance."

"True," he agreed.

The white officer looked at Mya. "Do you have someplace that you can go for the night?"

"Yes." She didn't waste any time answering the question.

"Okay. Well grab your things and we'll drop you off." Mya rushed into the room and packed her clothes.

\*\*\*

Tweety had just put AJ down for the night in the spare room that now belonged to him. Normally, the toddler knocked out early, but he had a cold. Therefore, he was cranky and it was difficult to get him comfortable.

Watching the sleeping child made her smile. He was a handsome little fellow with his smooth brown skin and low haircut. AJ and Jamir were the spitting image of their father. Tron couldn't deny the baby once Mya gave birth to him and sent him pictures.

Being a mother was never on Tweety's list of things to do. Let alone helping Mya with her motherly duties. To be quite frank, she didn't think she could have children.

When AJ was a few months old, Tron would call complaining about their living situation and how he didn't want Mya's drug addicted mother raising his son. Hearing about his baby mother's living arrangements made her feel sorry for the girl. Tweety had also come from an environment where drugs made her life hell. That eventually led her to sleeping around and finding comfort from older guys when she was in middle school. Tweety's mother couldn't keep her pussy on a leash, even if she tried.

A sudden knock at her door caused her to jump. Random visitors was not something she was used to. Tweety walked out of the bedroom and went to the living room. There was another knock, but this time it was a little harder.

"Who the fuck is this?" she mumbled, while looking out the peephole. The figure was clearly a man, but she couldn't see his face. And she knew it wasn't Tron because he wasn't being released for another two weeks. "Who is it?" she shouted.

"The police, open up."

"What?" Tweety whispered with confusion and placed her hand over her chest. In silence, she mumbled a prayer in hope that she wasn't about to receive any bad news.

Unlocking the door, she opened it up to see not only one officer but two, and they had Mya. "What's going on?"

"Do you know this young lady?"

"Yes. Mya, are you okay?"

"No," she mumbled.

The white officer was actually a sight for sore eyes and he had the prettiest teeth. "We responded to a dispute at her residence. Apparently, her and her mom had gotten into a fight. We don't think it's a good idea for her to be at home right now. Can she stay here?"

"Sure."

"If you don't mind me asking, what's your relationship to her?"

"Um. She's the mother of my stepson."

The officer cut his eyes and the black officer cleared his throat once they heard the nature of their relationship. "And you're sure she can stay here?"

"Yes. I have her son. He lives here with me. It's okay." Tweety extended her arm. "Come on, Mya."

The officer who was talking to Tweety stepped to the side, so she could walk in between them. "Thank you, ma'am. I guess we'll be on our way. Have a good night."

"You too."

Tweety closed the door and walked over to the sofa where Mya was sitting. There were scratches on her face and arms. Her lip was busted with dried blood on it. That alone made her feel bad for the teen. No matter the situation, she was still a child and didn't deserve that treatment.

"Mya, what happened?"

Embarrassed, she shook her head. Then she wiped the moisture from her eyes. "She was high and upset because I didn't bring her any cigarettes. Then she got mad when I said I wasn't paying her any rent when she has a live-in boyfriend. After that, she started fighting me. The neighbors called the police and here I am."

Tweety grabbed a pillow and held it in her arms. "Damn, I'm sorry you had to go through that. Paying rent should be the least of your worries right now. Focusing on school is more important than anything."

"Too bad she not thinking like that."

"What are you gonna do?"

"I don't know. I have some money saved. I'll just find me a room for now." Mya started to remove the remaining weave tracks in her head.

"No. You can stay here for a little while and I'll help you find a place of your own."

Mya appreciated the offer, but she couldn't accept. "You don't have to do that. You're already helping me with AJ. I wouldn't feel right living here. Me and my best friend discussed getting a place together, so I'm going to call her tomorrow."

"Okay, but in the meantime, you can stay."

"Thanks. I appreciate everything you're doing for me. I don't know any woman who would do any of this. I'll be out before Tron gets out."

"Don't worry about him. He'll be alright."

"I don't know. He acts like he hates me."

"Tron just doesn't know how to talk to people. Let me worry about him though. In the meantime, go clean yourself up. I know AJ is going to be happy to see you when he wakes up."

Mya got up and smiled. "Thanks, Tweety."

"You're welcome." Tweety was feeling tired so she went into her room to retire for the night.

# Chapter 6

Detective Terrell Andrews sat quietly in his office going through the surveillance tape he pulled from his cousin Terry's house. He had been watching footage for hours, so his eyes had grown tired. He was on the verge of nodding until he saw two females walk through the door. It was hard to make out their faces due to the grainy footage.

From what he could see, their encounter was friendly and then they disappeared into the kitchen. Not once did he blink until he saw them reappear sometime later. There was something certainly fishy about what he was looking at. "Maybe they set him up. I know damn well these two women aren't capable of murdering you so heinously."

In Terrell's mind, the murder was far too brutal for it to be women alone. Based on his experience, heinous kills stimulated from men and the women were the accomplice. Anxious to get to the bottom of the crime, he fast-forwarded the video until he saw a female figure resurface hours later.

The woman appeared to be having a conversation on the phone. "Yeah, open the door. Show me who you called."

Terrell was certain his assumption about a set-up was about to be confirmed. Then suddenly, she appeared startled, based on the way she ran back to the bedroom. Terrell scratched his head in disappointment. "What the hell is going on?"

It was upsetting and mind boggling that he couldn't see the last fatal moments of his cousin's life. Had there been cameras in the room, he could've solved the case in no time. As the video continued to play, Terrell tapped his pen against the wooden desk. His nerves were getting the best of him.

Not even a minute later, he could see the women enter back into the frame. The only difference was they weren't walking, they were running. Even with the four-second delay, it was obvious. Apparently, something went wrong. Terrell pressed rewind and watched it again. That time he determined they were carrying some sort of bag.

"A robbery," he mumbled. "If I don't catch you bitches, my name ain't Terrell Motherfucking Andrews. I'll retire my badge if I don't get justice for my cousin." Terrell pressed pause and picked up his cellphone.

"Hello."

"Hey, Glenn. It's Terrell. I need a favor from you."

"What's that?" Glenn automatically knew a deed needed to be done whenever he received a call from the crooked detective.

"I need you to pull a number and get the phone records for me. It's important."

Glenn pushed the rim of his glass further onto his nose. "I can do that, but you know it's going to cost you at the time of service."

"No problem. I'm willing to pay anything."

"Hmm, sounds urgent."

"It is. How long?"

"Give me a few hours." Terrell gave him Terry's number so he could get to work.

After hanging up, Terrell locked his computer and stepped out the office. He was in desperate need of a coffee break. The slight crack in the case had him on edge. To his surprise, the breakroom was empty and there was still a pot that was hot and ready. Picking up a cup, he filled it halfway and added creamer. Placing it to his lip, he took a sip.

"Can I have some?" He could feel a set of small hands roam his washboard stomach. There was no doubt about who was standing behind him.

"How do you want it?"

"Strong and black," she giggled.

Terrell turned around to face Marsha. She stood five-seven and weighed a solid one hundred and eighty pounds. Definitely thick in all the right places. Marsha was an attractive light-skinned broad with red freckles. "Is that right?"

"Yep. But you knew that already." Marsha rubbed the crotch of his pants and licked her lips. "So, can I expect you at my apartment tonight?"

"Is that an invitation?" He took another sip of his coffee.

"Of course."

"I think I can make that happen."

"Do that." She leaned forward and licked his ear. "I have a new nightgown I would love for you to see."

"I'll be there."

"Okay."

Terrell drooled as her ass jiggled like Jell-O when she walked away. Marsha had given him a hard on just that quickly. Now he was anticipating seeing her ass bounce while she rode him. Before he left the breakroom, he adjusted his meat in his pants. After waiting four hours, Terrell had finally received his cousin's phone records. He was that much closer to solving his murder. Carefully, he scanned through the call log to see the last call that was placed. There were two calls back to back, after midnight, that caught his attention. Using a special system on his computer, he was able to trace the number. The name came back to a Laneisha Huntley. Terrell marked down her last address and logged out of his computer. Terrell had his very first lead. Certain he had the suspect, he headed out the office to hunt her down. Inside the undercover car, he punched the address into the GPS system and started his journey.

***

Dazzle pulled up into Lala's apartment complex and parked in the designated guest area. It was delivery day for them and she had been nominated to be the driver. The door was unlocked, so she walked right in.

"Heyyy, whore! Let's go," Dazzle shouted throughout the apartment when she didn't see her present.

Lala entered the living room dressed in a pair of tight fitted jeans, a half-shirt that revealed her flat stomach and a pair of heels. "Why you so ghetto?" she laughed.

"Bitch, we grew up in the ghetto or did you forget that?" Dazzle looked her up and down and shook her head. "Why are you wearing heels, hoe? We making deliveries, not going to the club. Put on some Nikes or something."

"For what?" Lala tooted her nose up like something was rank in the air. "We dropping off drugs, not selling them on the corner. Besides, I need to be cute just in case I meet somebody."

"Don't you have somebody?"

"Now you already know the status of me and Honcho's arrangement." Lala opened her bag and placed her Glock .40 at the bottom of it.

"If you say so. You know these nineties babies crazy as hell. They don't care about shit."

"Bitch, we are nineties babies."

"I'm talking about the boys."

"Honcho know what it is and that's all that matters." Lala grabbed her bag and keys. "Let's go."

On their way to the car, a black on black Dodge Charger rolled past them slowly. Both ladies tried to peek inside, but the tints were extremely dark. "That might be a snack in that car." Lala giggled.

"Well, I have a whole man at the house. I'm not looking for no damn snack."

"Good for you, 'cause I am since we had to get rid of mine." Lala climbed into the passenger seat.

"If my memory serves me correct, I saved your life. And I'm still nervous about that shit. You haven't heard anything about it?"

"No. And I plan on keeping it that way, so don't think about it. Block that from your memory before it pops up. We're in the clear."

"I hope you're right, because I can't afford to go to jail and leave my son out here motherless."

Thirty minutes later, they pulled up to a house in Dillard. There were a few guys sitting on the porch. Lala and Dazzle stepped out the Infiniti and walked towards them.

"Damn!" The dark-skinned dude with a mouth full of golds was the first one to acknowledge them. He wasn't ugly, but he wasn't the best looking one out there either. "Who y'all is?"

Ignoring his question, Lala stood with her hand on her hip. "We looking for Boo. Is he here?"

"I'll answer your question after you answer mine, sexy." Judging by the black tint on his lips, Lala could see he smoked all the weed.

"I'm the supplier. Now, where is Boo?"

"Oh, damn." He covered his mouth with his hand like he was surprised. "Damn, I ain't know it was a chick. My bad, baby. Let me open the door for you."

"Thank you." Lala hit him with a phony smile.

"Damn shorty, you can get it too," he said, when he checked out Dazzle and the way her jeans hugged her just right.

"No thank you. I'm happily taken."

The women stepped inside the house and Lala took the lead. They were then greeted by a handsome, brown-skinned stranger with gold teeth and long dreads. His taper and beard were sharply trimmed like Steve Harvey. Lala was certain he was the man in charge, based on his expensive threads and jewelry. Sexy was an understatement.

"I'm going to assume you are Boo."

"And you'll be correct." He flashed her with a million-dollar smile.

"I'm Lala and this is Dazzle."

"Nice to meet you, ladies." Boo reached for Dazzle's hand first. Then he grabbed hers. *Oh yeah, he's interested*, she thought. The smell of his cologne invaded her nostrils and melted her panties. Lala knew she wasn't tripping when he caressed the palm of her hand for a long period of time. Finally, he released it. "Have a seat."

Boo sat in the loveseat and picked up a black bag from the floor. Slowly, he removed several stacks of neatly wrapped bills and placed them on the table. "That's forty-five grand."

Dazzle picked up the bills and started to count them. Lala then removed the three kilos from her bag and sat them in front of him. "Three keys as promised."

Boo picked up a knife and cut a slit in each package. Then he tested the substance using a small tube with liquid in it. Lala paid close attention as she watched the liquid turn light burgundy. That was something she had never witnessed before. Therefore, it made her wonder what the result meant, but his response gave her the answer she needed.

"Oh yeah, that bitch potent."

"Did you doubt us?" Lala couldn't resist being sassy with her new handsome client.

"Not at all. It's just business."

"Just checking." Lala continued to blush.

Dazzle had just finished counting the last stack of cash. "It's all here."

"It was nice doing business with you." Lala stood up and extended her hand. This time, he kissed it.

"Likewise. See you soon."

Boo stood to his feet. "You promise?"

"That depends on you and how fast you need me to come back and pay you a visit."

"I'll be in touch," he assured her.

"Okay."

"Nice meeting you, Dazzle." Boo walked them to the door.

"Likewise."

Lala and Dazzle left the house feeling accomplished. That was their first drop-off of many more to come.

# Chapter 7

## Okeechobee Correctional Institution

Tweety sat anxiously in her Nissan Maxima, waiting on Tron to walk out into the free world. It had been a long-ass, three and a half years and she was happy it had come to an end. It finally felt good to say goodbye to collect calls, letter writing, visitations, strip searches and commissary. All she wanted was for him to commit and do everything he promised from behind that wall, while be confined to that little ass cell.

Their plan was simple. The future was mapped out. It was written in stone. All Tweety had to do was get the work from Tori and pass it along to him. In return, he would sell it and turn a profit in order to take care of his makeshift family.

Forty-five minutes had passed, and Tron still hadn't been released. Tweety was antsy and ready to see her man. She had lost count of the amount of times she checked the time on her phone. Just as Tweety was about to call inside the building, she saw a familiar figure walking through the exit doors.

Tron stepped onto the free soil, looking dapper in his Ralph Lauren 'fit and crispy Air Force Ones. Tweety didn't hesitate to emerge from the car like it caught a fire. Running full speed towards him, she jumped into his arms once she was close enough. Tron spent a lot of time doing bench presses, so Tweety was lightweight in his arms.

"Baby, I'm so happy to see you." She planted multiple kisses on his face. "I missed you so much."

"I missed you too, baby." Tron placed Tweety back on her feet. "Come on, let's get the fuck off these people property. I done spent more than enough time here."

Halfway down the road, Tron glanced in the back seat like he was looking for something. "I see you didn't bring my lil nigga with you." Slight disappointment weighed on his voice.

"I know and I wanted to bring him with me, but I changed my mind at the last minute. I remembered I wanted to get in a little time before we made it back to this hectic house."

"Damn, it's that bad?" Tron rubbed his head. "You mean to tell me I'm about to step into some drama?"

"No. Not like that. I'm saying that because AJ is a busy body and he craves attention." Tweety glanced over at him, unable to contain her excitement. "You might as well get ready, 'cause I know he's going to be all over you."

Tron couldn't wait to make it back to his hometown. He was ready to hang out, turn up and fall knee deep into some pussy. "I'm definitely ready for his bad ass." Then he thought about his firstborn that was missing from the picture. "I need to see Jamir. I miss him so much."

"Good luck with that," she hissed.

"Dazzle pussy ass gone make me fuck her up. My mama told me she just started back bringing him around, but not the way she used to."

The sound of Dazzle's name made her cringe. Tweety was upset as if the shoes were on the other foot and her ex best-friend slept with her man. "Well, you know how selfish and spiteful she is. All she doing is using Jamir as a pawn."

Tron bit down on his bottom lip. Just the thought of her keeping his son away ate away at his flesh. "It's all good. I'm home now and I'mma beat that bitch ass when I catch her. I owe her for the old and the new."

"That's not a good idea. You're just getting home and we don't need any more drama in our lives."

"When it comes down to my seed, I don't give a fuck about none of that. I haven't seen my boy in years except through fucking pictures," Tron snapped.

"Okay baby, relax. I'm just saying I want you to stay out of trouble, that's all."

Tron wasn't trying to hear none of that irrelevant shit. He wanted to see Jamir and if that meant he had to bury Dazzle in order to do it, then so be it. "Where's your phone?"

"In my purse."

Tron retrieved her phone and placed calls to all of his homeboys that rode his sentence with him. Lastly, he hit up his old girl just to check in. "Hello."

"Hey, Ma, I'm on my way to you." It felt good to finally say those words. Besides Tweety and his homeboys, his mama held him down for dear life. That served to be his greatest blessing.

"Hey, baby. I can't wait. I was wondering when you were going to call me."

Tron laughed. "Ma, we spoke damn near every day in there. You know I'm not missing a step."

"Better not." Sheila could hear an object crashing against the floor, so she turned her attention to the living room. "AJ, you better not be in there tearing up my damn house. Where is your mama?"

"Ma, what he doing?"

"Knocking over my candy jar on the table." Sheila walked into the living room to see Mya was no longer in there with him. AJ sat the small statue on the floor when he saw his grandma was in popping distance. "You want Nana to pop you?"

AJ shook his head no.

"His mama over there?" Tron scratched his head.

"Yeah."

"Oh," he replied.

"Why, is it a problem? You shouldn't have gotten her pregnant if you didn't want to be bothered with the girl. You need your ass kicked for fucking on a damn minor anyway."

"Nah, Ma. Chill out, I'm just asking."

"Okay."

"I'll see you soon, Ma."

Tron hung up the phone and placed it on his lap. Then he leaned back in the seat to enjoy the remainder of the ride. Minutes passed and the car was completely quiet. The silence was getting the best of him, so he decided to spark up a conversation.

"You alright over there?"

"Yeah. I'm good."

"Why you so quiet then?" Tron knew the answer to that question, but he needed to ask anyway.

"No reason. I'm good. Just trying to let you make your calls in peace."

Tron leaned over to the driver's seat and rubbed her thigh. Although she was upset with him, his welcoming touch still sent electricity up her thigh and into her honey well. "I'm sorry. It's just that I get pissed off whenever I think about what she did to me."

"I get that, but don't take it out on me."

"Yeah you right and that's why I apologized."

"I heard you." Her response was dry.

"Well, gimme a kiss." Tweety slightly turned her head, so he could put his lips on hers.

Per his request, she wore a loose-fitting dress for easy access. Tron's slender fingers took a slow drive to the honeycomb hideout. Slowly, he fondled her clit. Once she was nice and wet, he slipped in one finger, then the second. Using his gentle, circular motions on her clit, he tapped on it periodically. Tweety exhaled deeply, while he took her on a ride of his own. Every ten seconds, he would slip inside and beckon a come-hither motion with his finger. After a few minutes of the repetitive action, she released her sticky fluids onto his fingers. Tron drew his hand back and licked the remaining juices.

"Mm. Mm. Good. You getting pregnant tonight." Tweety was blushing hard, while watching him suck his fingers clean. The spell he cast on her made Tweety forget she was mad in the first place. She couldn't wait to get home so they could make love all night, but first they had to go to his mother's house for a surprise barbeque.

***

"Damn, I got me a real-life Bonnie," Jude smirked, while gripping Tori's backside. He kissed her lips as he stared at the keys of coke on the table. With her help, there was no doubt the couple could rise to the top and take over. "Queen of the muthafuckin' trap."

"Live and in the flesh, baby." Tori stepped from his warm embrace and walked over to the table. "I just need to get rid of these last ten so I can re-up."

"I'll make a few calls and see if my boys need some work. I know my brother needs three keys since his connect went MIA, and my cousin need a quarter." Jude stroked his chin.

"Good, 'cause I wanna get rid of this work as quickly as possible. I'm still in the process of bringing on more clients." Tori picked up her keys and purse from the table.

"Where you headed?"

"I'm about to go and meet up with this guy I know from Parkway and make him an offer."

Concerned about his girl's safety, he offered his help. "I can ride with you if you like."

Tori could hold her own and she didn't need anyone to accompany her for this particular meeting. "No. It's okay, baby. I got it. You can go ahead and do what you need to do about this work. I'll be okay."

"Okay. I'll be checking in on you to make sure you good."

"I know I'm not going to win this." Tori pecked him on the lips. "I'll see you later."

***

Tori arrived at her meeting thirty minutes later. Normally, she would take Honcho along with her, but since she had a personal relationship with her potential client, she decided against it. Riding solo was her best option. As she stood in front of the door, she knocked three times.

"Who is it?" the voice asked from the other side of the door.

"Tori."

The door opened and Deon stood there looking sexier than ever. Standing at an even six feet, he was shirtless and drenched in sweat. His biceps were bulging and so was the print in his basketball shorts. Tori did her best not to look.

"Hmm. Is this how you dress for your business meetings?" Tori giggled.

"Only for you." Deon stepped back so she could walk inside. "So, Miss Tori, how have you been? I haven't seen you in years."

Tori sat down on the forest green leather sofa. "I've been good. I was in Atlanta for college, but I'm back now."

"You graduated?"

"Of course."

Deon smiled at his longtime crush. "I'll be right back. Make yourself at home."

Tori sat and waited patiently, but Deon reappeared within five minutes. He was still shirtless, but he was dry now. "Let me get a hug."

Tori stood to her feet and gave in to his request. "So, what have you been up to?"

"You know me, working and hustling."

"That I know." Tori wanted to get right to business, so she continued. "The reason I wanted to meet up with you is because I want to be your new supplier."

Deon knew the purpose of the meeting, but he wasn't aware of the full details. "So, you back working with your dad? 'Cause you know that's who I get my work from." He wasn't asking a question. He was making a statement.

"Yeah. I know that, but I've branched off and doing my own thing." Tori leaned forward and killed the smile, so he'd know she was serious. "And I also know you paying eighteen bands for a key. If you shop with me, I'll give you a key of uncut raw dope for fifteen."

Deon thought for a second. "That's a good price. So, Diesel good with me copping work from you?"

"Let me worry about my dad. Do we have a deal?" Tori asked. There was no need at beating around the bush. She needed an answer and she needed one now.

Deon thought long and hard about the business proposition. It sounded good, but he didn't want any heat coming his way. He ran a smooth, solo operation and that was the way he wanted to keep it. As he continued to weigh his options, he thought about the fact that he could get closer to Tori. He had always had a crush on her and maybe that would give him a shot at being her nigga. With a smirk on his face, he smiled.

"We have a deal."

That made Tori happier than a sissy with a bag full of dicks. "I knew you would see it my way."

"A new shipment will be in shortly, so I'll be in touch."

"Sounds good to me."

\*\*\*

The knock on the door caused Jarvis to jump to his feet nervously, while clutching his piece of steel. Life on the run was stressful, but he had to stay on his toes. Cautiously he approached the door and peeped through the peephole. Once he saw a familiar face, he took a deep breath and opened the door. The relief he felt was unexplainable.

"Whaddup, cuz?" Jarvis dapped up his first cousin on his mother's side of the family.

"Shit, just cooling and making this money. I can't complain." Jude walked inside the house and sat his Louis Vuitton backpack on the table. Getting comfortable, he sat down on the sofa and put his feet up on the table. "What you got in this bitch to smoke?"

"Some gas."

"Roll up then." Jude pulled the work out his backpack and placed it on the table. "I got that work for you."

"Good looking out, fam." Jarvis pulled out a Swisher Sweet and rolled up.

"Good looking out, my ass. Run me that cash."

"Damn, fam, I got you in a few days."

"Nah nigga, tonight." Jude folded his hands and straightened his face so his baby cousin knew he was serious.

"You fucking the plug, can't you wait?"

"Hell, nah. You ain't about to fuck up what I got going on. I'm good on that."

"Damn, for real?" Jarvis' brow raised slightly because he couldn't believe what he was hearing. "You would've never met the bitch if it wasn't for me."

"Watch yo' mouth, fam. I love Tori."

Jarvis shook his head and chuckled. "This bitch got you pussy whipped, I see. It's cool. Let me get you your money." He dropped the blunt on the table and stood up. Then he went into the room to get his stash money for his re-up. Upon his return, Jude was rolling up the blunt he started.

"Here."

Jude thumbed through the bills and smiled. "That wasn't so hard, was it?"

"You got it." Jarvis knew he didn't want any problems with the menace of the family. The reputation he held was a murderous one. Jude would never hesitate to drop a body and he didn't want to be a victim. It was clear Tori had put her voodoo pussy on him and fucked up his judgement. Clearly, he was off track, but there was nothing he could do about the killer that sat in his living room.

# Chapter 8

Two hours later, Tweety pulled up in front of his mama's house in Wilton Manors. To his surprise, the yard was packed with his family and friends. "Ooh, shit. You knew about this?" Tron laughed, as he rocked in his seat with brightly lit eyes.

"Yes. It's a welcome home barbeque." Tweety turned the car off and they got out.

On the way up, Tron was greeted with a friendly hug by his childhood friend, Jeff. "What's up, my boy? I'm glad to see you out."

"It's good to be back," he smiled.

"I'm going in the house." Tweety rubbed his shoulder and went towards the front door.

Jeff was one of the homies that held him down and dropped off money to his mama during his bid. The two were more like brothers than anything. He rubbed his hands together with a devious smirk on his face. "So, what's up for the night? You trying to go out and get in the world?"

"Nah, bro. Tonight, I want to chill with my family and my girl. We can link up over the weekend and it's whatever."

They dapped it up once more. "Let's slide in the back so you can see your mom."

The layout of the house had changed since the last time he stepped foot into his old girl's house. It was laced with new, red leather furniture and a gold glass table. Tron was taken aback when he noticed the photos of him and his children inside a white and gold matching china cabinet. As Tron moved forward to get a closer look, movement to the right of him caught his attention. Standing a few feet away from him was Mya, and he couldn't believe the way she transitioned into a full-grown woman. She'd sent him a few pictures in the beginning, but then she stopped halfway into his sentence.

"Hey, Tron." Mya's voice was low and her eyes never left his.

"Hey, Mya. How you been?" he asked.

"I'm good. Glad to see you free."

"It feels good to be free." Tron couldn't resist looking at her small, thick frame. The baby definitely filled her out in all the right places. Her ass had even gotten fatter. "Can I get a hug?"

"Sure." Mya nervously stepped into his embrace. She could feel the firmness of his chest, along with the scent of his cologne, and that alone made Mya blush and her panties wet.

Tron remembered Tweety was somewhere near, so he released her from his grip. "Where's my son?"

"He's out back playing with the kids."

Tron looked around the room to see who was looking at him. When he realized everyone was doing their own thing, he gripped a handful of pussy through her jean shorts. "You gone let me get this again?"

Mya's heart rate began to beat rapidly from his touch. She wanted to just melt right there, but she had to restrain herself. Instead, she pushed his hand away. "Tron, stop. You have a girlfriend and I live with her."

"Damn, it's like that? You don't love a nigga no more, huh?" Tron was trying his best to bait her.

"It's not about that. You have a woman and I'm not about to cross that line with her. She's been good to me. It would be different if y'all wasn't together."

"I feel you." Tron held his hands up in surrender. "My bad."

Mya exited through the front door to go and gather her thoughts. She still loved Tron. That went without saying. The problem that lay between Mya and Tron was Tweety. As long as she was in the picture, there was no future for them. Nor was she willing to engage in a sexual relationship with him. Mya did that when he was with Dazzle and in the end, that led her nowhere fast. All Tron gave her was a baby she loved dearly and a broken heart that caused so much resentment.

After being shot down by his baby mama, Tron made his way to the kitchen. A familiar aroma tickled his nose and made his stomach growl. He rubbed his belly. "Oooohhh, wee! These collard greens smell so good."

Sheila's chestnut-colored eyes landed on her baby boy, as she held him tightly in her arms. "I'm so happy to see you. The Lord answered my prayers. I missed you so much."

"I missed you too, Ma." Taking a step back, he took a good look at her beauty. At fifty-two years old, Sheila still looked youthful, as her cinnamon skin glistened against the lighting. "Where's AJ?"

"He's outside."

"Thanks, Ma. I appreciate everything you did for my kids while I was away."

Sheila scrunched up her face and exhaled. "I did the best I could do. That damn Dazzle hasn't brought Jamir over here in months. I don't know what's wrong with that girl."

"Me either, Ma, but I'mma handle her though. I'm not about to let her keep me away from my son no longer than she already has." Tron rubbed his hands over his face. "I can't stand that bitch."

Sheila grabbed her son's hands. "I know you're frustrated, but you know I didn't raise you to disrespect women. Even though she's not acting like a woman, still show her some respect. At the end of the day, you cheated on her with Mya and had a baby. So, you contributed to this drama that's going on."

"Don't take her side. There's a lot that Dazzle did and I'm sure she didn't tell you about it. She only told you what she wanted you to know."

Sheila placed her hand on his cheek. "Baby, I know. I was a young girl before. All I'm saying is, respect the mother of your kids. Try reaching out to her so you can see my grandson."

"I will," he agreed.

"Antron." She only called him by his government when she was upset or giving him a life lesson. "I don't want to hear about you getting into any trouble or putting your hands on her. Leave that girl alone. Focus on seeing your son and getting yourself together."

"I'm not gone touch her. I promise."

Sheila picked up the dish cloth and proceeded to wipe the counter. "And I don't understand why you with Tweety. She's a good person and all, but that was Dazzle's best friend. You were wrong for that."

Tron peeked out the window and when he saw Tweety sitting down at the table, he was relieved. "The situation with her just happened. I was trying to be a family man, but Dazzle kept pushing me away. Nothing I did was good enough."

"Sounds like the blame game to me. You need to accept accountability for your part in your relationship ending. And any woman that's willing to lay down with her best friend's man ain't no good."

"I did. I get that sleeping with Tweety was a mistake, but in the end, she was there for me when I needed her the most."

"That doesn't mean you have to be with that person and besides, how can you trust her?" She stopped wiping the counter and looked into his eyes. "The thing about mistakes is that we learn from them and we grow from them. If you still want to be a family man, change your ways. You have a second chance to get it right. Don't miss out on the opportunity that's staring you right in the face."

Tron thought about what she said, but he didn't respond. Instead, he kissed her cheek and followed the sound of the music playing outdoors. Tron was greeted by a large welcome home sign and a yard full of friends and family. Some were dancing, playing cards, dominos and his younger cousins were in the corner smoking weed. He could smell the potent aroma in the air.

"Nephew!" Tron hugged his uncle. "It's been a long time, boy."

"I know, right? That was the last time. They won't ever see my black ass again."

"Better not, 'cause you got two fine ass women out here." Unc took a sip of his malt liquor. "You bad, nephew."

"It ain't like that, Unc."

"I hear you, young blood, but I know better." He patted Tron on the back. "Gone out there and mingle, we have plenty of time to chop it up."

The barbeque ended a little after nine that night. Damn near everyone was tipsy when they left, except the elders. Tweety was in the house nursing her headache, while Tron stood on the side of the road, talking with Jeff. The old friends were joking and kicking the shit. Suddenly, Mya appeared from the side of the tree, talking on the phone. That immediately caught Tron's attention. He could've sworn he saw her leave a while ago.

Jeff laughed at the hungry look in his boy's eyes. He knew what time it was. "You trying to smash that ain't cha, boy?"

Tron grinned. "Fuckin' right. It's that obvious?"

"Yeah, nigga. You gotta get the slob off your lip." Jeff flicked his bottom lip.

Tron moved his head back. "Watch out, nigga. I don't know where your hands been."

"On deez nuts," he laughed.

"Aye, Mya! Come here." Tron was tipsy, horny and he needed some pussy bad. True enough Tweety was in the house ready and willing, but he wanted Mya. Especially after the conversation he had with his mother. He put his back against the truck and looked in her direction.

"I guess I gotta be the lookout." Jeff took a step to the right so he could get a full view of the front door. There was no way he was letting his boy get caught.

Mya pushed her phone into her back pocket and sauntered towards the road with her hand on her hip. "What's up?"

"Come here."

Slowly, she moved closer to him, but she left a few inches between them. It was almost like she was afraid to get too close. Shaking his head, he bit his bottom lip and grinned. "Come here, girl."

Tron grabbed her wrist and pulled her into his arms. "Why you playing with me?" His hands maneuvered over her curves until they landed on her soft ass. "I see you got fine for me."

Mya wanted his attention, but not at the expense of having her heart broken again. "Why you doing this and Tweety in the house?"

"Stop worrying about Tweety, and worry about me and you."

"Tron, there is no me and you. We have a son and that's it."

"Damn, it's like that?"

"Yes. You have a girlfriend."

"Since when did that matter to you?"

"Let me go." Mya tried to wiggle her way out of his strong arms.

Tron refused to comply. Forcibly, he pushed her against the truck and leaned against her small frame. Using his right hand, he grabbed the front of her shorts and unsnapped the buckle. Mya could smell the alcohol and weed on his breath. And she was sure her breath smelled the same. "Tron, stop. Please," she whimpered.

"Nah. You belong to me and I need you to remember that." Tron shoved his hand inside her panties and massaged her clit. The aggression with his touch turned her on. Mya closed her eyes and leaned her head against the window. There was no doubt he made her feel good. Shifting her leg, she planted her foot on the truck's side rail to give him easy access. Tron's fingers slithered in and out of her wetness. Her juices seeped from her opening.

"Sssss! Ahhh!" Mya couldn't resist. She placed both hands on his face and kissed his lips. Tron reciprocated and slipped his tongue into her mouth. "I want you to fuck me now," she whispered. Everything she stood for went out the window.

"Oh, we definitely fucking." Tron pulled his hand out of her shorts and licked his fingers. Looking down, he grabbed his stiff rod. "See what you do to me?"

For the first time all evening, she smiled. "I see. So, what we gone do about Tweety?"

Tron grabbed the bridge of his nose and laughed. "Tweety out for the night."

"What you mean?"

"My mama gave her two of her pain pills. That ass out for the night. So, it's just me and you, baby."

Curiously she asked, "Where we going?"

"Aye, Jeff."

Jeff walked from the opposite side of the truck. "Whaddup?"

"Let a nigga use the spare room for a few hours."

"You got it. Let's slide."

They got into Jeff's truck and drove five blocks over to his house. Tron escorted Mya to the bedroom and closed the door. By the time he locked it and turned around, Mya was completely naked and on all fours.

"Damn, baby mama." Tron took off his shirt and then his wife beater. The view of her plump lips from the back made him rock up instantly.

Tron crept up behind her and thumbed the middle to get her back wet. Leaning forward, he licked up and down her slit before slurping heavily on her pearl. Tron's pole was about to burst through his pants, so he took them off and threw them to the floor.

Stroking his piece, he slid into her slippery twat with no hesitation and pumped in and out. "Damn, baby mama. This pussy still good and tight."

Mya leaned forward until her chest was resting against the bed. But she kept her arch strong, no matter how deep he rammed inside her guts. "Fuuuck!" she screamed. "Ssss. Ouuuuu. Tron! Tron!" she moaned repeatedly, like his name was the chorus in a song.

Tron squeezed her cheeks and spread them open, so he could watch his heavily coated meat slide in and out. "You don't know how many nights I laid on my bunk, thinking about getting up in this pussy again."

The strong grip she had on him threatened a premature nut, so he pulled out and slapped it against her ass. The second the tingling stopped, Tron got up on the bed and planted his feet on the mattress. Back inside her warm spot, he beat her down with a vengeance. Tron held the small of her back and squatted in the pussy like he was a frog.

"Oh my gosh. Oh my gosh, it's in my stomach. Ah! Ah! Ah!"

"Unh-huh. I know you been out here giving my shit away." Tron smacked her ass hard. *Whap*! The wetness and lethal strokes caused her pussy to fart uncontrollably. "Yeah. Talk to me. That pussy talking to me."

Tron could feel heavy pressure in his stomach and at the tip of his head. But this time he wasn't stopping it. He needed to feel that nut. Seconds later, he released a heavy hot load into her stomach. When he was finished, he laid down on the bed. Mya crawled up beside him and tongue kissed him. "I missed you."

"I missed you too, but we ain't finished yet. Get him back up with them sexy ass lips and ride my shit backwards."

"Okay." Mya got up, took his rod in her hand and did exactly what she was told. She had to show him what he'd been missing. "Welcome home baby."

# Chapter 9

Tank, Ace and Max rode in silence as they got off on exit 29A, better known as Sunrise Boulevard. That particular area was heavy into drugs. If they weren't selling it, they were using it. It was the perfect spot to set up and run shop. Lauderdale was known for their tricked-out cars, candy paint, rims and loud music that shook the ground like an earthquake.

To the left at the gas station, a group of dudes was posted up with their expensive whips. Tank grinned, as looked towards the crowd. "These niggas lucky I'm on a mission, 'cause I'll make them bitches lay down," he laughed, while holding up his chopper. "I'll make this bitch dance all over Sunland."

"That's my fuckin' brother," Max shouted from the back seat. "Make them fuck niggas do a hundred-yard dash," he continued to hype him up.

"They ain't gone know what hit they ass." Max sat his weapon in his lap.

Ace whipped the steering wheel onto tenth terrace and proceeded to the corner store. Out front there was three dudes posted up kicking the shit and laughing. They were so heavy into their conversation, they never noticed Tank and Max creep up on them until it was too late.

"I heard y'all boys over here making money."

The short nigga with the big head pulled his hands out his pockets and frowned. "Who you though? And why the fuck you asking all these damn questions?"

Max was two seconds away from spazzing the fuck out. It was clear that young fool hadn't checked his resume. "Normally, I would light a bitch nigga up for disrespecting me, but I'mma let you slide right now." Max took a deep breath. "Anyway, nigga, I'm about to offer you the opportunity of a lifetime."

"Oh yeah, what's that?"

Max slapped the young nigga's chest with the back of his hand. "You can keep your turf and hustle for the winning team. We about to have all this shit on lock, so if you wanna continue to make money on this block, you'll make the right choice."

"And what if I say no?" he folded his arms across his chest.

Tank pulled the chopper from behind his back. "Then your family get to have a fish fry and wear your face on a shirt next weekend."

The other two boys stood there in silence, but Big Head was nodding and rubbing his chin as if he had to think hard about living or dying. "Listen homie, I don't know who sent you, but I'm not interested. This my hood and ain't nobody moving shit over here unless Diesel approve that shit."

Tank raised the chopper and made it dance. *Fraaaack! Fraaaack!* Big Head's body rocked hard, as the bullets made a home in his body and hit the ground. His white tee was now soaked with red blood. The two boys stood at attention. Fear rushed through their veins.

Tank was now staring them down. "The same offer applies to y'all, so what's it gone be? Y'all rockin' with the team or you laying down with this dummy?"

"We rockin' wit' y'all," they replied.

"I thought y'all would see it my way. I'll be up here tomorrow after I let my boss lady know you niggas on board. It'll be business as usual, so don't make me look for y'all. If you buck, I'll kill your whole family, Zack and Harold. Don't think I don't know where you live at."

Both boys were stunned to hear the stranger drop their names. Tank and Max jumped back into the car and sped off. It was time for their next mission. They had four more spots to hit before they called it a night.

Once the car was out of close range, Harold and Zack took off running down the block. Safely at their residence, the two ducked off into the backyard. Zack sat down on a crate to catch his breath. Harold remained on his feet.

"Aye, you don't recognize them niggas?"

"Hell, nah." Zack was still out of breath.

"Man, I can't believe that nigga killed Head." Harold sat down on the other crate and ran his hands through his small afro. "These niggas gotta pay."

Zack sucked his teeth. "Oh yeah? Well, how you plan on doing that? You heard what that nigga said."

Harold wasn't too keen on his cousin acting like a bitch. "You act like the boss ain't got clout in these streets."

"If he had that much clout, niggas wouldn't be trying to take over his spot."

"We'll see about this shit once I tell Diesel what the lick read." Harold couldn't wait to put his boss up to speed. One thing for sure, he wasn't going back up to that store unless Diesel sent reinforcement.

\*\*\*

The following afternoon, Harold sat on his front porch smoking a cigarette and waiting on Diesel to pull up at any second now. Last night's events were still playing with his mind. Head was more than a friend. He was more like a brother. The two had been friends since the days of hide and go seek. Revenge was heavily on his mind. Etched in his brain, but he didn't know where to start, being that he had no idea who the shooter was or where he was from.

Coming up the sidewalk, he saw one of the neighborhood girls twisting and making bubbles with her gum. "What's up, Harold?"

Harold moved the Newport from his lips and flicked the ashes into the grass. "Shit. Chillin'."

"I heard about Head. They still have the block roped off." Harold nodded his head and took another pull from his cigarette. "Sorry for your loss. I know y'all was close."

"Thanks."

"So, you was with him last night? I heard you was."

"Who said that shit?"

"Now you know the streets talk. I don't know who said it, but my best friend told me that's what she heard."

"Nah. I had done left already when that shit went down."

The sight of the black Suburban, pulling up caught his attention. Flicking the cigarette, he rose to his feet and pulled up his pants. "I'll holla at you later. I gotta go."

"Alright."

Harold walked up to the truck and got into the backseat. Diesel was sitting with his legs crossed and a mean mug on his face. Intimidation wasn't the word to describe the way he was feeling at the present moment. "What was so urgent that you needed me to drive here?"

"Shit fucked up right now," Harold sighed, as the vicious murder replayed in his head.

"Explain."

"Last night we was posted up at the store getting to the money. Then out of nowhere, three niggas pulled up with straps. They talm 'bout join the winning team or get laid the fuck out. Head told the nigga in charge nothing moved without your say-so and the nigga blasted him in the chest."

"Who the fuck is these country ass niggas?"

"Ion know. Never see 'em before." Suddenly, Harold remembered what the shooter said. He shook his finger. "Aye, that nigga did say his boss was a bitch tho'."

"A bitch, huh?" Diesel's eyes lowered to the floor.

"Yeah. He never said her name."

"A'ight. I'mma look into who behind this new organization, because whoever it is must be new to the game. And they can't possibly know who I am."

"That's what I'm saying," Harold agreed. "What you want me to do?"

"Why you not dead? What did you tell him?" Diesel knew there was only reason Harold was alive, but he needed to hear the answer from the horse's mouth.

"I told them niggas I was rockin', shit. Ain't no need for me to die for no reason."

"Then do just that. See if you can find out who she is. In the meantime, I'll do my own research on this and get back with you." Diesel checked the Rolex on his wrist. "Don't fuck this up. If you hear something, make sure you call me pronto."

"I won't fuck this up. But these niggas gotta pay for what they did to my boy."

Diesel cut his eyes in Harold's direction. "I just said don't fuck this up. Once I get the info I need, you can do whatever you want. Until then keep your composure and pay attention."

"Got it, boss."

When Harold stepped from the truck and closed the door, Byrd looked in the rearview mirror at Diesel. "You know what this means, right?"

"I do." Diesel stroked his beard.

"You know who behind this, right?"

"I have an idea it's that daughter of mine."

"So, what we gonna do about that?"

"First, I need to confirm it's really her, before I make any rash decisions." Diesel pulled out his cellphone and scrolled through the call log.

"We been down this road before and you know she not gone tell you." Byrd was trying his best to make sure his friend was listening carefully.

"Pull off," he barked.

Deep down inside, Diesel knew Byrd was right. He thought he was able to make Tori shake her dope girl ambitions, but it was obvious he was wrong. Many nights, his mind wouldn't let him rest, because he knew Tori was behind stepping onto his territory. She was even responsible for the hit on the warehouse years ago, but she was his flesh and blood. His firstborn. His one and only girl. Diesel didn't know how to handle it, because his baby girl had his heart. Then, on the other hand, he felt like it was time to teach her a valuable lesson in the game of life. If she wanted to be a queen pin, it was time to treat her like an enemy. His emotions were mixed, but something had to be done. Tori was making him lose money and he couldn't have that.

# Chapter 10

### Two weeks later

Tori stepped out from the passenger seat, dressed to the nines in a tight-fitted, royal blue business dress. On her feet were a pair of multi-colored pumps that complimented her attire. Adjusting her designer frames, Tori stood on the sidewalk with her hand on her hip. Jude closed the door for his lady and grabbed her hand.

"You ready for this?"

"I was born ready."

Standing in front of her newly purchased storefront was a line of applicants, waiting for an on the spot interview for her hair store, Bianca's Hair Boutique. Tori was happy with the turnout. She just hoped there were qualified, honest individuals amongst the crowd.

Tori stood in front of the glass and unlocked the door. The start of her own legitimate business was a dream come true. The place was decked out in purple and gold. The epitome of royalty truly fit for a queen. Glass cases filled with jewelry, accessories and hair weaves were up against all four walls.

"Who's coming up to help you interview?" Jude locked the door behind them.

"Lala's coming. She should be here any minute now."

"Is there anything you need me to do?"

Tori thought for a moment. "No. You can leave if you want to. I'll be tied up in here for a while."

"You strapped?"

"Does a baby wear diapers?" she giggled.

"I should've known."

"You know my strap goes wherever I go."

Jude grabbed Tori by the hips and pulled her close. "That I know." Leaning forward, he planted a wet kiss on her juicy lips. The slip of her tongue made it tantalizing.

Tori broke their kiss and took a step back, while licking her lips. "Whew! Stop right there. I don't need you getting me all hot and bothered and not do anything."

Jude loosened his belt buckle. "I mean, you do have a back office we can utilize for a few minutes."

"Baby, you know that's not happening, right? I have people outside waiting on me. But, don't you worry, you can get all of this good loving later on tonight."

"I'll be looking forward to that." He licked his lips.

"I know you will."

Jude's curious eyes were glued to her chest. He then reached out and grabbed the diamond piece on her necklace. "What's this?"

"My wedding ring."

"You and Kilo were married?"

"Yes." Tori tried to read his straight face, but it didn't help. It was hard to detect how he was feeling. "Does this make you uncomfortable?"

"Honestly speaking. No. It doesn't." Jude recognized the sudden sadness in her eyes and grabbed her hand. "I'm not a jealous dude, baby. If it makes you feel better wearing it, then do that. I'll never tell you to remove it, until I'm ready to replace it."

"Thank you for being so understanding. That means so much to me."

A loud knock on the door caused the couple to swivel their heads towards the entrance. Jude shook his head. "I know damn well them muthafuckas ain't being impatient."

"That's Lala."

"I got the door." Jude had a smooth walk and swag, like Barack Obama.

Lala stepped inside with a huge smile and wide eyes. She was definitely glowing. "Girl, did you see that long ass line out there? Bitch, everybody and they mammy need a job, I see." Tori and Lala embraced in a sisterly hug. "I'm so excited for you."

"Thank you. I appreciate you coming here to help me."

"Girl, you don't have to thank me. You my sister. My best bitch. I'm your ride or die for life." Lala twerked in place with no regards to the man standing before her.

"Why you so damn stupid?" Tori laughed. "Anyway, this is my boyfriend Jude."

"Nice to finally meet you, Jude. It's nice to see she brought you out of hiding."

Jude laughed heartily at her comment. In his mind, he could tell Lala was the character out of the group. "I guess I proved myself, since she just introducing us after all this time."

"It has not been that long, stop it." Tori playfully slapped him on the arm.

"I know. I'm joking, baby." Jude kissed her on the lips. "I gotta go, baby. Call me when you ready." Then he reached out to hug Lala. "It was nice to meet you."

"Same here," she smiled.

Lala waited until Jude was out of the store before she turned her attention back to Tori. "Girl, why he look finer in the daylight? You better keep his ass."

"Oh, I plan on it." Tori smiled as she watched him get into his car. "He ain't my husband, but he's close enough."

"I heard that. But you already know there will never be another Kilo, baby."

Tori twirled the diamond ring in between her fingers, as she stared at the walls. "Never."

"You ready to start these interviews? 'Cause I know them people hot as fuck out there."

"Yeah. Go ahead and let in the first applicant."

\*\*\*

Tron walked through his mother's front door a little after noon, with Jeff on his heels. Tweety, his mother and son, were all sitting in the living room watching a kiddie show. His lady's arms were folded and her lips were tooted up. Right off the bat, he knew she had a major attitude with him returning the next day. To avoid a confrontation in front of his mother, he played it cool.

"How you feeling, baby?" Torn leaned down and attempted to kiss her lips, but Tweety dodged him faster than a curve ball. Instead of her face, they landed on her cheek.

"Where have you been?"

"Man, this nigga had me all over Lauderdale, getting drunk and hanging with the homies. Don't be mad at me."

Jeff was quick to come to his boy's defense. "It ain't his fault, sis. Blame me. He told me he had to go home, but I didn't pay that no mind. I missed my brother, that's all."

Tweety didn't want to show her natural black ass in front of his mama, so she kept it ladylike for the time being. She mustered up a fake smile. "It's cool. Don't sweat it. I'm not upset," she lied.

"A'ight, bro. I'm out. Hit me up later on." Jeff gave Tron a G-hug and left.

Tron grabbed Tweety by the hand. "Come on. Let's go. I'm ready to go home and get in the bed. I'm tired as hell." Without a reply, she stood to her feet and picked up her purse.

"Y'all can leave my grandbaby here with me. Pick him up tomorrow."

"Nah, Ma. I'm home now. I got him."

"Just go home. He'll be okay. I promised my baby I'll take him to the store to get a toy. I know you want some privacy."

Tron thought about what she was insinuating and agreed. "Well, we'll pick him up in the morning." He picked up AJ. "Daddy will see you in the morning, man. I love you." AJ kissed his daddy on the cheek, before trying to leap from his arms and into the arms of his grandmother.

"We gone, Ma."

The minute Tweety pulled out the driveway, she ripped Tron a new asshole. "Now that we are out of your mother's presence, where the fuck have you been? And I don't want to hear no bullshit ass story about you being with lying ass Jeff."

Tron swiveled his head in her direction quickly. "Man, what the fuck you talking about? The man just sat there and told you what happened. I was trying to come back, but he wouldn't drop me off. What the fuck you wanted me to do? Jump out the car and walk back?"

"Yep. You could've called me and I would've picked you up."

"Yo ass was sleep."

"Exactly, I was sleep. Not in no fucking coma." Tweety shook her head and tried her best not to cry. "You think I'm so fuckin' stupid."

"You trippin' for real. I don't wanna go through this shit on my first day out. Damn, chill the fuck out. I came home to you and I'm with you now. Be grateful for that."

Tweety slammed on brakes at the yellow light. Normally, she flushed on through, but Tron had her fucked all the way up. "Grateful? Nigga, grateful for what? You out here cheating on your first day out. What the fuck I got to be grateful for?"

"Cheat? Are you fuckin serious? Who in the hell I could've possibly fucked that fast?" Tron kept a straight face as he lied through his wolf teeth.

"Any one of these Broward hoes."

"Listen, I haven't did shit. So, stop accusing me. All I did was chill with my boys and get drunk. That's it."

"Okay. If you say so."

Tweety turned the volume up and hit the gas hard, the second the light turned green to get on I-95. At the top her lungs, she sang along with Beyoncé, as "Resentment," bumped through her speakers, her eyes glued to the road.

"I wish I could believe you, then I'd be all right. But now everything you told me really don't apply. To the way I feel inside. Loving you was easy once upon a time. But now my suspicions of you have multiplied and it's all because you lied."

Tron sat in the passenger seat, laughing and shaking his head. She was really doing the most, in his eyes. Granted, her assumptions were true, but she had no proof. He continued to glance in her direction but didn't say a word. If she wanted to act crazy, he wasn't going to interrupt her tantrum. But as she got into the song, her tears finally began to flow, so he decided to power off the stereo.

"Why you did that?" she snapped.

"'Cause you bugging for real. A nigga ain't even do shit."

"You goddamn lie."

"If that's what you wanna believe, then go ahead. You already have your mind made up."

"Yep." Tweety turned the stereo back on, but Tron was sick of that sad ass song, so he turned it off again.

The Atlantic exit was coming up, so she waited until she veered off the highway to turn it back on. Tron wasn't trying to hear it. He turned if off again. There was an all-out battle after that. The disgruntled couple fought over control of the stereo, as the car swerved.

"Man, watch the fuckin' road before you kill us."

"We gone die together then."

"Yo' muthafuckin' ass crazy. Watch the road, silly ass girl."

"Fuck you, Tron."

By the time Tweety looked up, she was gunning it behind the car paused at the red light. Instantly, she slammed on brakes, but the car slid slowly and bumped the car in front of her.

"Look at this shit. I told your silly ass to watch the fuckin' road." Tron was furious with her stupidity.

The passenger in front of them jumped out with an angry scowl on his face and his arms in the air. At a fast pace, he walked to the rear of the car to check the damage. Then he walked towards their car. Tron jumped out to diffuse the situation before it started.

"What the fuck? You didn't see us sitting here, my nigga?" the angry man snapped.

"My bad, bruh. My girl wasn't paying attention." Tron checked out the damages for himself, but realized it wasn't anything more than a small bump, because the bumper was still intact.

"Shit, she need to be."

"I know that, but there aren't any damages. So, what you wanna do?"

"What I wanna do? Fuck you mean?"

The woman who was driving was now standing beside him, grabbing his arm. "Errol, just relax. There's no damage. It's all good. Just get in the car."

"Nah, fuck that. This bitch should've been paying attention to where the fuck she was going." Errol was heated.

Tron did his best to remain calm. The last thing he needed was an altercation on his first day out. "Listen, bruh, I get that you upset, but what we not gone do is start with the disrespect. It was honestly an accident. Now if you wanna handle this in another way, I'm 'bout that too."

Tweety got out the car just as the woman stepped in between them to keep the two men from fighting. "Sir, just get in the car, it's okay. Errol, let's go before you go to jail for nothing." Thinking for a brief second, he walked off and got back into the passenger seat.

Tron got back into the car and so did Tweety. He ejected the CD that was playing and tossed it out the window. "Why did you do that?" she shouted.

"Just drive the damn car. You done already fucked up my buzz with this kiddie ass shit."

"And I wonder why."

Ten minutes later, they were home and his baby mama wasn't there, to Tweety's surprise. Tron walked straight into the bedroom. He was truly tired from his long night with Mya and sick of the battle with his woman. All he wanted to do was sleep and recuperate. However, sleep was farther than he thought. Tweety walked in behind him like a raging bull, as he climbed into the queen-sized bed.

"I know you don't think you about to go to sleep." She stood beside him with her hands on her hips.

Tron laid on his back looking up at the ceiling. "Didn't I tell yo' ass I was tired?"

"I don't give a fuck about what you said. You ain't going to sleep until I tell you to."

"If you was gone be on this fuck shit, you could've left me at my old girl house. Girl, you must be crazy. I spent all them years in the chain gang listening to bitches and niggas telling me what to do. I'm in the free world now and nobody can't tell me shit. Them days over with, sweetie."

"Tron, don't play with me. I'll fuck you up. I'm not Dazzle." She placed her knee up on the bed. "And speaking of which, did you see Jamir?"

Tron opened his eyes and looked directly up at her. "Now we getting to the bottom of the real problem. That' what this is."

"What?"

"Just go ahead and ask me if I fucked Dazzle last night. That's what this is all about anyway."

Tweety didn't hesitate to throw out the real question at hand. "Well, since you brought it up, did you fuck her? Is that who you were really with last night?"

"I haven't spoken to Dazzle. Neither has my mama. That girl don't even know I'm out."

"You sure about that?"

"You asked a question and I gave you an answer. Now leave it alone. I don't need to lie about seeing my baby mama." Tron closed his eyes, so he could tune her out. The same way he did with the noisy niggas in prison.

"Oh, she your baby mama now. Yesterday in the car, she was a bitch. That's funny."

"I bet it is. I'm going to sleep."

"Whatever," she replied.

Tweety was so mad she left the room and went to take a shower. By the time she returned twenty minutes later, Tron was still on his back and fast asleep. Tossing her towel onto the dresser, she removed the bonnet from her head and locked the door. "He got me fucked up if he think we ain't fucking," she mumbled.

Briskly, she walked towards the bed and started to remove his shorts. Tron didn't move a muscle. Tweety smelled his rod before stroking it and placing his limp piece into her mouth. There were no traces of another bitch's pussy juice, so she slowly bobbed up and down for a few minutes. His body wiggled a bit, but he never opened his eyes. Satisfied when he finally reached his full length, she climbed onto his lap and slid down his pole. Tweety was in full control, as she rode him until his hands made their way to her ass.

Tron was well aware of what was going on. His drunken state was long gone. She killed that during the ride home with the unwanted bickering. Blinking a few times, he chuckled.

Tweety managed to whisper between moans, "What's funny?"

"You."

"Why?"

"You just swore me up and down I had my dick buried deep in another bitch, but you just sucked my shit with no problem."

"Shut up." Her hands were planted onto his chest, as she grinded hard on his rod. "Ah! Sss. Ooh."

"If this was all you wanted, that's all you had to say." Tron bit down on his bottom lip and grabbed her breasts with both hands.

After making Tweety sweat it out for a rough ten minutes, he flipped her over and dipped his stick into her Hershey highway, and beat her down until she admitted who was in charge.

# Chapter 11

The sun began to fade away, as darkness threatened the once sunny sky. The black truck cruised at a slow pace up the block of 27th Street in Collier City. There was a small crowd present. They were drinking and smoking right in front of the corner store. Byrd pulled the truck into the second parking spot on the side of the building and put it in park.

After sitting for five minutes, Byrd spotted the dude they were looking for. "You want me to go and grab this nigga?"

Diesel was staring out the window at their target. "Yeah."

Byrd immediately hopped out the truck and walked up into the crowd. His mean mug made it easy to tell he was about business. Diesel watched him exchange words with the young hustler before they walked towards the truck together. Once they were inside, Diesel didn't bother to turn around. He remained facing the front as he spoke.

"We about to take a ride." His voice was low, yet stern.

"Okay," Marcus replied. In the back of his mind, he had a feeling he knew what the pop-up visit was about, but he wasn't about to speak until spoken to.

The truck was silent for the fifteen minutes it took to arrive at the warehouse in Deerfield. Byrd parked the truck and they all got out. Marcus was escorted to the office. Diesel sat down at his desk and leaned back in the seat with his hands folded.

"I'm sure you don't know why I brought you here, but I'm going to enlighten you. I'm going to ask you a question and I need for you to give me an honest answer. Can you do that?"

Marcus nodded his head. "Yeah."

"Are you selling dope for my daughter?" Diesel was blunt and straight to the point.

"Nah." He didn't hesitate with the lie he fed him.

"See, what I don't like is a liar."

"But I—"

Diesel cut him off completely. "I didn't tell you to speak. You need to listen before you answer me. Now, I want to let you in on a little secret. If I ask you a question, it's because I know the answer already. One thing I can't stand is a liar and you already off to a bad start." He then nodded in Byrd's direction.

Byrd moved swiftly behind Marcus and put him in the chokehold. "Now, he's going to ask you again and this time you better answer correctly, nigga."

"This time you better answer correctly, or the next time your family sees you will be at the coroner's office, identifying your mangled body. Now, again, I'm going to ask you if you are selling dope for my daughter Tori." Diesel leaned forward and placed his thumb on his chin and fingers on his lips.

The answer didn't come fast enough, so Byrd used his right hand to pull out his pocketknife, open it and place it against his neck. "I think he asked you a question. This is where you need to answer, unless your body is ready to part ways with your head."

Marcus thought about the danger he was truly in. As much as he wanted to protect his crush, his life was a tad bit more valuable than her secret. "Okay, okay. I'll tell you."

"Spill it before I spill your guts onto this floor," Byrd threatened the young hustler, but he was serious as they came. And to prove that, he pressed the sharp knife against his Adam's apple until he broke his skin.

"Yes. Yes. I sell dope for her. She recruited me to hustle in the Pompano area."

Diesel moved his hand. "See, that wasn't so hard now, was it? Now, I have another question. Who is her supplier?"

That was truly a question he couldn't answer. But somehow, he knew that was where his next problem lay. If he couldn't produce a supplier, there was no way they were going to let him walk away alive.

"I don't know."

"I call bullshit, D." Byrd kept the knife at his neck.

"Yeah, I can smell it on this nigga." Diesel opened the desk drawer and pulled out an army green, Smith and Wesson nine-millimeter handgun. "I'm tired of playing games with you. If you can't tell me what I need to know, you get to die here, right now."

Marcus started to beg for his life. "Please don't kill me, man. I don't know who she deals with. We not close like that and she'll never tell who her supplier is. That's crazy. Think about it. Why would she tell us who she getting dope from? That girl smarter than that and you know it. You raised her."

Diesel sat his gun down. Everything Marcus stated was the truth. Tori was a certified hustler and she learned from the best. Him. So, there was no way she would disclose that type of information.

"I'm going to take your word for it this time."

Marcus couldn't take any chances at leaving his woman and kids behind for something he knew nothing about. "I'm telling the truth. I don't know who her supplier is, but I will say that her and Honcho are pretty close. He's working for her and I'm sure he knows who her supplier is. That nigga is her right hand and bodyguard."

Diesel's ears perked up. If Honcho was working for her, that meant one thing. "Honcho? You talking about Eazy's son, Honcho?"

"Yeah."

Diesel cut his eyes at Byrd. "Take him into the spare room and tie him up." Then he looked back at Marcus. "If your story checks out, I'll let you go. If not, when we return, I will let him carve your skin, layer by layer, until you tell the truth or we hit a bone. You got that?"

"It's the truth. I'm not lying to you. I'm just trying to get back to my family. I promise."

"Okay. We'll see about that." Diesel sat back in his seat and contemplated his next move. If what Marcus was saying was correct, he was closer to locating Tori's supplier than he originally expected.

***

### The Next Day

Lala bagged the keys of coke for her delivery, as Tori sat at the kitchen table of her new spot, sipping on a cold bottle of champagne. Zipping up the bag, she peeped her sister eyeballing her heavily with a somber expression on her face.

"You good, baby?"

"Yeah. I'm just thinking."

"About what?" Lala sat down, preparing for a long talk. It had been a while since they had a heart-to-heart and it was long overdue.

Tori took another sip from her wine glass and took a long, deep breath. "I've been keeping so much bottled up and I feel like I'm about to fucking explode."

Lala could sense the seriousness in her girl's voice. It had her deeply concerned. "You know you can talk to me, Tori. We don't keep secrets. We've been friends over ten years, so tell me what's up."

"My life is fucked up. I'm miserable and sometimes I feel like taking my own life." Tori teared up as soon as those words left her mouth.

"Bitch, you at the top of the food chain right now. I don't know what could have you so down. You living—" Lala stopped herself midsentence and walked to the opposite side of the table. "Is this about Kilo?"

"Yes." Her voice elevated to the highest capacity. "Me and Kilo supposed to be at the top right now and raising our baby. But I'm at the top and I feel so alone."

Lala put her arms around Tori and hugged her tight, while stroking her hair. "We all know ain't nobody kill Kilo, but some hating ass niggas. Show these niggas what Kilo taught you and ball out on these broke ass niggas who act like bitches."

"No. No," she cried.

Lala grabbed Tori by the face with both hands. "Yes. You have to do that. It's what he would want."

"No," she continued to cry. "You don't understand."

"What don't I understand?"

"It was. It was." Her words were stuck in her throat, but she had to get it out by any means necessary. The burden was too much for her to carry alone. "It was Diesel. He killed Kilo."

"That can't be true. I know he hated him, but he had no reason to kill him."

"Lala, it was him. Eazy told me. He found out and tried to kill my dad." She held onto Lala for dear life.

"He told you he tried to kill him?"

"He's going to kill him."

"Damn, what you gone do?"

Tori shook her head. "There's nothing I can do." Pausing briefly, she looked up at Lala. "Besides, he took away the love of my life. He's the reason I'm suffering now and he deserves to suffer too."

"I can only imagine how you feel. I'm here for you and don't you forget that. You don't have to keep secrets from me."

"That's not even the half of it. Diesel brought his girlfriend and son with him to my graduation."

Lala took a step back and held up one hand. She was trying her best to understand what the hell she was saying. "Wait! What?"

"Yes. He has a seven-year-old son I'm just finding out about."

"Seven?" Lala blurted out.

"Yes. That means he was cheating on my mom and had that baby. I swear, I hate his guts and I don't give a fuck what Eazy does to him. But I am going to ask him about his role in Kilo's death. I need closure and he needs justice. That's the only way I can go on in life."

"I'm so sorry. This is a lot to take in and I know it's hard on you." Lala had a few concerns of her own and now was the best time to address it. "Can I ask you a question?"

"Anything."

"Do you think you're truly ready to date another man? You're not over Kilo and I think you need more time to heal. He's been gone four years, and you're still mourning and wearing your wedding ring."

"I know, but the fact of the matter is I'll never get over him." Tori raised her glass from the counter and took a sip. "And this thing with Jude just happened unexpectedly. I had no intentions on dating and he just showed up out the blue to serve as a distraction."

"Just take your time with him. I haven't heard anything about him, but you know I'm concerned about you to say the least."

"Thanks. I do feel a little better now that I got that off my chest." Tori stood up and hugged Lala once again. "Go ahead and make your delivery because I'll keep you all day."

"What you about to do?"

"Meet up with Tweety. She hit me up about wanting to work for me now. I guess her money is low."

"You sure you want that hoe to work for you? That bitch foul as fuck."

"I get that. But if she can get rid of this work, then hey, I'll give her a chance."

"I'm telling you now, she got once chance. If she do anything slimy, I'm fucking her up."

"That's cool, 'cause after that I'm killing her." Tori giggled, but she was dead ass serious. "See, a bitch like Tweety, you have to keep her close. You control the money... you control the bitch. Believe me, I'm not fucking with her like that. It's strictly business and that's the only relationship I'll ever have with her."

"Be careful with that hoe, seriously, because I don't like this shit."

"You know I pay attention. I'll be cautious with her. You have my word. But anyway, get out of here. You know Boo waiting on you."

"See you later. Love you."

"I love you too."

***

Tron took a shower after Tweety left to meet up with Tori. He was excited that his days of petty hustling were behind him and he was about to embark on a more lucrative business. With the dope Tweety was about to get from her girl, he had plans on supplying his boys and a few gits from the hood. Standing in the mirror he brushed his teeth and washed his face.

"You a handsome nigga boy and in a few months, you gone be eating in these streets," he smiled at himself.

The sound of his new phone ringing snatched him from his conceited talk about himself. Jeff hooked him up with a phone and three grand to get on his feet. Sprinting down the hallway in only a towel, he ran into the bedroom and picked up the phone.

"Wassup, my boy?"

"Shit. What you doing?" Jeff asked.

"Just getting my ass out the shower. Wae you at with it?"

"At the crib. You coming out?"

"Hell, yeah. I ain't staying in here with this crazy ass girl all day. This muthafucka retarded."

Jeff was cracking up on the other end of the phone. "What the fuck happened?"

"After we left my old girl house, all she wanted to do was bitch and moan about me cheating." Tron walked into the kitchen to fix himself a sandwich. "And I ain't on that shit."

"Well, that's what you was doing." Jeff laughed again.

"I know that, but she don't know that. Then she playing all this crazy ass music, so I turned the radio off. I wasn't trying to hear that shit. Then her crazy ass trying to stop me, and not watching the road and ran into the back of somebody car."

"Damn, bro. That shit crazy."

"Who you telling?" He opened up the fridge and took out some lunchmeat and mayo. Then he went over to the counter and sat it down. "Then, I'm about to get into it with the nigga in the car on some bullshit. She just do too much."

"I feel that. When you ready, hit me back so I can come and scoop you up. We getting in the world today, for real."

"Hell, yeah. She went to meet up with her girl to grab what we talked about."

"Oh, that's what's up. A nigga like me ready to pump up on these bitches and niggas."

"I already know."

The sound of the door unlocking alerted Tron. He looked towards the living room. "Damn, she back fast."

"Who, Tweety?"

"Yeah." The front door opened and in walked Mya, wearing a short ass dress that left nothing to the imagination. That was an instant turn-on for him. "Aye bro, I'll hit you back when I'm ready."

"A'ight, fool."

Tron hung up the phone and looked in her direction. "Where you been?"

"With my homegirl, why?"

"'Cause I need to know. Come here."

"For what? I'm not your woman."

"Stop playing with me. You still belong to me."

Mya rolled her eyes and walked towards him. "If you say so."

"Let me ask you a question." He leaned against the counter still wearing his towel. "What the hell made you come stay here?"

Mya stood directly in front of him. She was so close she could feel his meat through the cotton towel. "I wanted to be closer to you. So, one night after work I started a fight with my mama and somebody called the police on us. I knew she would feel bad and let me stay."

Tron wrapped his arms around her tiny waist. "You had this all planned out, huh?"

"Yep. Are you surprised?" she smirked.

"Yeah, but I don't want you staying here."

Mya's eyes widened in surprise, so she moved his hands. "Oh, I see what it is."

"No. I don't mean like that." He put his hands back in place.

"Well, what do you mean?"

"You need your own place, so I can come over there with you and my son."

"I can't afford to pay anybody's rent, take care of myself and the baby," she huffed.

"I'm out now. You don't have to worry about that anymore. I got you and our son."

"We'll see."

"I'm serious. I'm about to link up with Jeff after I get this work and start back hustling. I got you. Just go find a place ASAP."

"I need money for that. Do you have money for me to move out?"

"I just said I got you. I'm about to give you two thousand dollars and I want you to go and find a place."

"When?" She folded her arms and shot him a curious stare.

"Right now. I have the money in the room."

"You moving in?" Mya desperately wanted a relationship with the father of her child. Therefore, she was willing to do whatever it took to get him. When Tron didn't respond, it bothered her deep down in her soul. "I guess that's a no."

"No. It's not. I have a lot to handle before I can commit to that. Tweety was there for my bid and I can't just up and leave her like that."

"Oh, but you can leave me alone with our son. You have no ties with her. Y'all don't have no kids."

"Just chill." Tron raised her dress. He smiled when he realized she wasn't wearing any panties. "You wore this for me?"

"Nope."

"Mya, stop playing with me. I'll beat your ass. And after today, I don't want to catch you in no more skimpy shit like this. Nobody should be able to look at what belongs to me."

"Tron, I don't belong to you."

"We'll see about that."

Mya felt cool air travel up the crack of her ass. "Put my dress down please and finish making your sandwich."

"Fuck that sandwich. I found something else I wanna eat." Tron switched positions with Mya and pushed her against the bottom cabinet.

Mya was ready for whatever Tron was on, but she would've preferred it to not be in Tweety's house. But hell, it wasn't like she hadn't done it before. Besides, she couldn't turn him down and piss him off. It was important that Mya proved she wanted him just as much as he wanted her. Even if that meant sleeping with him in the home of the woman who helped her during his incarceration.

Swiftly, Tron picked Mya up and placed her on the counter. Pushing her legs open, he took a nosedive into her goodies and sucked her soul from her body. Mya placed her hands on top of his head and slipped into ecstasy.

# Chapter 12

Standing inside the walk-in closet, Diesel pulled his purple Polo shirt over his head and fixed his collar. He could feel a set of eyes on him, so he turned around and came in contact with Jenna. She was standing at the door with her arms folded.

"Where are you going?"

"Out. I have business to handle."

"Did you forget what you promised us today?" Her face carried a less than happy expression.

"No. I didn't forget, but again, I have business to handle first. Therefore, you have to wait until I'm done with that." Diesel grabbed his weapon and tucked it into the waistband at the back of his pants.

"Fine." Jenna turned to walk away, but he stopped her.

"Get back here and tell me what the problem is!" he demanded with bass in his voice.

"It's nothing, Diesel. Go handle your business and I'll be right here waiting on you, as usual."

"That's what you're supposed to be doing anyway. I moved you in here, so you'd stop thinking I have bitches running in and out my house. To show you I want to be with you. But of course, that's not enough for you. If you want to move back to Weston, then I can arrange that. Other than that, go find you something to do."

"Oh really, that's how you feel? You don't want me here."

"Stop putting words in my damn mouth. You heard exactly what I said." Diesel brushed past her. Money needed to be made and he didn't have time to entertain her insecurities.

"I'm so sick of this shit. Maybe I should start doing what the fuck I want to do. You ain't gone be satisfied until I give another nigga this pussy."

Something clicked in Diesel's head, causing him to snap. Grabbing Jenna by the throat, he slammed her against the wall with a great amount of force, causing it to vibrate. "What I told you about saying that? You better watch your fuckin' mouth, before I rip out your tongue. That's not for you to say, so choose your words wisely and I'm not saying it again. And the day you decide to fuck another nigga, will your last day on earth." Diesel gave her a hard push. Jenna's body collapsed against the dresser. "Now write this down. I fucked up my relationship with my daughter to be with you. She might never forgive me, so don't ever disrespect me like that again, or I'll do you just like I did Bianca."

By the time Diesel made it downstairs, Byrd was standing at the front door waiting on him. "What's eating at you?"

"Bitches, bruh."

"I should've known. Deal with her when you come back. In the meantime, push that shit out your skull. We have shit to do and I need your head in the game."

"I'm good. Let's ride."

Diesel sat in the back seat of the truck and called Tori's phone. As expected, she didn't answer, so he tried a few more times. On his fourth attempt, she picked up with an attitude brewing through the line. "Yeah."

"Why I have to call you so many times for you pick up? Not too long ago, you loved me when you thought I was dead."

Tori was not in the mood to talk to him, but she didn't really have a choice, since he was living on borrowed time. "I'm going to be honest with you. I don't feel like you and I have anything to discuss. You ruined my mother's life and my life and you think I'm supposed to forgive you? I'm sorry, but I can't. You committed the ultimate sin, because of your selfishness."

Diesel was a little confused by the accusations. "Tori, baby. What are you talking about? If you think I ruined your life by sending you away to college, then so be it. I can accept that. All I wanted was for you to have the best in life."

"Tell me this, did you kill Kilo?"

The question caught him by surprise, but he had to be quick on his feet. "No. I didn't kill him. What makes you think that?"

"There is no one on this planet that hated Kilo more than you. The sad part about it is that you didn't have a valid reason to do so."

"Tori, listen to me. I did not kill him."

"I don't believe you and until you can come clean and tell the truth, don't ever call me again. I'm no longer your daughter until you confess your wrongdoing."

Diesel stared at the phone screen once she hung up. He tried to call her back, but it went straight to the voicemail.

For the next thirty-five minutes, the truck was silent. The radio was even off. It was obvious someone had been whispering in Tori's ear and he had a feeling it was Eazy. "Yo, we need to handle Eazy as quick as possible. Tori questioning me about killing Kilo all of a sudden. I can't lose my daughter behind this bullshit."

"I heard." Byrd glanced towards the backseat through the rearview mirror. "Just tell her the truth."

"Nigga, is you crazy? I can't tell her I ordered my incompetent soldiers to kidnap him. My name needs to be far away from that as possible. She'll never forgive me for this one."

Byrd didn't say another word, as he pulled into the Coral Gables neighborhood and up into the driveway. After being granted permission to enter, he pulled up in front of the immaculate house and parked.

Diesel and Byrd stepped onto the porch and rang the doorbell. About a minute later, the door opened and his old partner was standing there in a robe.

"What's up, Diesel?"

"Goddamn Domino, I'm glad you could see me on such short notice." The two men G-hugged.

"Whaddup, Byrd?" Domino hugged Byrd as well.

"Maintaining."

"Come in. Come in." Domino stepped back.

The three men walked through the house and into the study and closed the door. "Have a seat." Domino sat behind his desk and crossed his legs. "Now, let me get this correct. You need a new supplier?"

"Yeah. My supplier just got hit and I have money to make. I don't have time to sit around and take losses. I'm not trying to operate without product for no amount of time. Anxious niggas flee the ship when it stops, and I can't have that."

"I can feel you on that. How much product we talking, though?" Domino was all for making money, so when Diesel hit him up, he didn't decline.

"I need two hundred kilos."

Domino rubbed his hands together. Those were his type of numbers. "And all I need is four million dollars."

Diesel's demeanor and face quickly turned sour. "Nah, I need the same price you give Tori."

"Tori?"

"Yeah. My daughter."

"Listen, what I did for your daughter was on the strength of Eazy and Kilo. So, what you not about to do is walk into my home and tell me what you gone pay. If that's what you thought, you can get the fuck out my house. Pronto! 'Cause this meeting is over." Domino stood up and fixed his robe.

"I think you better have a seat." Diesel nodded towards his chair.

"You've come to your senses?" Domino asked.

"Yeah."

Diesel waited until he sat back down before holding his left hand up and snapping his fingers. Immediately, Byrd pulled his heat from his waistband and aimed it at Domino.

"What the fuck you doing, man?" Domino was stunned by Diesel's actions.

"What made you think it was okay to have my daughter as your distributor? We don't cross those lines, old friend."

"I asked her why not use you as her supplier, Tori said she didn't want to mix business with family. But shit, at the end of the day, she grown and I didn't recruit her, she came to me."

"And you couldn't call me?" Diesel massaged his temple.

"You know that's the game, Diesel. It's nothing personal. It's all about the money."

Diesel stood up and placed his hands deep inside his pockets to get one last look at him. "And this is personal. I'll see you in hell, whenever I get there." Then he glanced at Byrd, who was twisting on his silencer. "Smoke this nigga." Byrd fired two shots, one in his head and the other in his chest. "Now let's go and free Marcus."

\*\*\*

Tori drove to Eazy's house after receiving an urgent text from him. Off top, she knew it had everything to do with Diesel. And at that point, she was confused as ever. With no solid proof that he pulled the trigger, there was no way to state a case. Tori's mind was made up, whatever Eazy decided to do, she would have to deal with it. Now, standing on the porch, she took a deep breath and unlocked the door. Securing the locks behind her, she roamed around the house until she found Eazy in his bedroom. The door was open, but she knocked as she stepped inside.

"Hey, Pops. What's going on?"

Eazy placed his phone on the nightstand, beside his pistol and stroked his beard, as he thought about the devastating news he received earlier. "Come here and have a seat."

Tori glanced at the gun, as she made her way towards him in slow motion and sat down. "What's wrong?"

"I received a call not too long ago that Domino was murdered in his own home earlier today."

"What?" Tori was completely disturbed by what she'd just heard. True enough, death came with the territory, but she wasn't expecting to lose her plug. "What happened?"

"Diesel and Byrd are behind this. They met up with him to have a meeting about product and after they were gone, his right hand went to check on him because he never came out. When he found him, he was dead from two gunshot wounds."

Tori was beyond disgusted. Diesel was yet again trying to destroy her empire. "I'm sorry. This is all my fault."

"No. It's his fault."

"Yeah, but if I would've stayed out the drug game, this would've never happened." The nature of it all was weighing her down. "I just want him out my life. I'm sick of him. I wish he would've died, instead of my mama."

That was music to his ears. Eazy was ready to take Diesel out once and for all. "Did you ask him about Kilo?"

"Yeah. He lied and said he didn't do it, but I know he did. My heart is telling me so."

"I'll handle him. Just stay away from him."

"It will be hard for you to get ahold of him, but I'll make sure that happens. Just give me some time to come up with a plan."

"I will. Just come by and let me know what the plan is. He done killed two people close to me. There won't be a third."

"Trust me, I have this under control. He has to pay for what he did." Tori stood up and hugged Eazy tight.

"Going forward, I'll be the new supplier. I spoke with my Mexican connect and he wants me to take over."

"That's good news. I'm almost ready for a new shipment."

"I got you covered."

On her way down the hall, she stopped in front of Honcho's room and knocked on the door. "Come in," he shouted.

Tori opened the door to find Honcho sitting in a chair playing the PlayStation. "What's up, little brother?"

"Coolin', sis. What's good?"

"You ready to head up to Atlanta and set up shop?" Tori sat down on the bed Indian style.

Honcho paused the game and turned to face her. "Hell, yeah. I done spoke to my homies up there and they ready to sell this shit."

"I hope so. I'm ready to expand. We can start with the weed first and then we can ease the dope in smoothly. It's a few niggas up there I know who trapping heavy, so I know I can get them on board."

"Sounds like a plan to me."

"We can leave in a few days. I just need to get some shit together before I do so. I'll keep you posted."

"A'ight, sis, do that."

"I'm headed home. See you later."

"Be safe."

"Always."

Tori headed out with a mountain of problems on her mind. Her heart was set on revenge. Kilo would've killed for her without hesitation and she was determined to do the same for him. But before it went down, she needed to get answers and then set a plan in motion.

Before going home, she stopped by Miami Subs, since she hadn't eaten all day.

As she sat in the drive-thru line waiting to place her order, she came up with the perfect idea. Picking up her phone, she scrolled through her contacts until she found who she was looking for.

"Hello."

"Hey, Whitney. This Tori."

"Oh, hey girl. How you been? I was wondering when you was gone call me, so we can link up." Whitney was happy her longtime friend called.

"I'm good. I've just been busy with my new business venture, that's all. Are you busy right now? 'Cause I need your help with something."

"Anything. What is it?"

"Is your uncle still with the police department?"

"Yeah."

"Can you arrange a meeting with him for me? It's important. I'll even pay you if you can make that happen."

"Sure thing. I got you. Let me call him and I'll hit you back in a few." Whitney worked as a correctional officer with the feds and she could use a few extra dollars.

"Okay." Tori smiled as she hung up the phone. If she could get him on board, then everything else would fall into place.

\*\*\*

## Sinaloa, Mexico

Charro stood in his office, two stepping, singing and puffing on a cigar. "Pocos amigos que son reales. Cuánto te halagan si tienes éxito. Y si fallas lo entenderás. Los buenos se quedan los otros se van," Charro sang in his native tongue. In plain English, it meant, few friends who are real. How much they flatter you if you are successful. And if you fail, you will understand. The good ones are left, the others leave.

91

The news about the death of his main distributor was quite surprising. True enough, it came with the territory, but the hassle of finding a replacement was what bothered him the most. He appreciated long lasting business relationships and he had been just that. Domino was also one of his reliable money makers in the states for years, with a clean pipeline and now he was gone.

The sound of his cowboy boots clunked hard against the floor. It followed by a hard knock on the door. "Come in."

In walked his number-two, Emilio, with the newest member to join his cartel. "You wanted to see me, boss?" The newbie looked at his boss with the side eye.

Charro laughed. "What's wrong? It's Julio Iglesias." He picked up the remote and turned down the volume on his stereo. "What's wrong, Lance? You don't like my music?" he smiled.

"It's not my cup of tea, but do you," he chuckled. From the day he met Charro, he had been nothing but a character.

"Maybe I can change your mind. Hmm?"

"I doubt it."

Emilio couldn't ignore the fact that his fellow mate was tied to a chair with a gag in his mouth. "What's going on in here?"

"Hmm, where do I start?" Charro walked over to Jose and removed the gag. "Jose here has a problem with putting his hands where they don't belong. Isn't that right, Jose?"

"Yes," he cried. "I can make it up to you though. Just give me a chance."

"No. No. If I give you a chance, then everyone will want a chance. We can't have that."

"What you gone do about that?" Emilio asked.

"He deserves a nice and quiet death. Nothing that goes boom or makes a big mess in my nice office. This rug cost me thirty thousand dollars." Charro bent down and picked up a thick piece of plastic and handed it to Lance.

"Would you do the honors?"

Lance took the plastic from his hand and stepped behind the chair. Jose was breathing heavily. Without a warning, he wrapped the plastic around his head and pulled it hard. His grip was tight. Jose kicked and attempted to scream. They all watched as the bag fogged up. Two minutes in, his movement slowed down as life began to slip from his body. The fact that he was young didn't bother Lance not one bit. It wasn't his first go-round. Applying more muscle, it took seconds for his body to go limp.

When it was over, Lance moved the bag and dropped it to the floor. Charro turned around and sat his cigar into the ashtray. "Have a seat." Emilio and Lance sat in the two chairs positioned in front of the cherry wood desk. Charro took his seat as well.

"As you both know, my number-one distributor was murdered and we need a replacement."

"Yes. I'm aware of that. What do you need us to do?" Emilio replied.

"I'm getting to that." Charro looked into the eyes of his new employee. "Lance, I know you're new here, but I feel like I can trust you. Over the past several months, you've proven yourself to me and Jose vouches for you."

Lance nodded his head. "I appreciate you taking a chance on me. I know it was hard for you being that I fled from the states."

"True indeed." He cleared his throat. "Just don't make me regret it. I have no problem with taking life from those that cross me. You see what just happened to my nephew?"

Lance couldn't believe that Charro had him to kill his own flesh and blood. It was obvious there were no rules in the game. Nor were there second chances to make amends.

"Tomorrow, I need the two of you to head back to the states and do a delivery to the new distributor, Eazy. He's to receive one hundred kilos. Travel will be by boat to keep a low profile and the coke will be in banana boxes. The Coast Guard off the coast of Miami will be awaiting your arrival. They've been paid, so you can pass freely. Be in and out." Charro shifted his eyes. "Lance, can you handle that?"

"Without a doubt. I can make that happen in my sleep."

Pleased with the response, he continued. "Be ready at seven in the morning to be dropped off at the docks."

"Okay," Emilio agreed. "Is that all?"

"Drop him off far away from my residence and call the policía, being that I'm about to have a grieving sister."

Lance stood from his seat and fixed his shirt. On his way out of the office, he thought about his return to the United States. It had been eight months since he arrived in Mexico, on a mission, and that was far too long to live in the most dangerous country known to man. He prayed it would be over soon, so he could resume life the best way he knew how.

# Chapter 13

Tron walked downstairs and hopped into the truck with Jeff. He was in the car smoking on some Kush. "What's good, my boy? I'm glad you finally coming out the crib."

"Yeah, I had to chill with this crazy ass girl before she lose her damn marbles."

"Sis is throwed off. You better chill out." Jeff passed him the weed.

"Sis better sit her muthafuckin' ass down somewhere. She knew what type of nigga I was before she got into this shit. Now all of a sudden, she want a nigga to be a muthafuckin' saint. Prison ain't change me one bit."

"I mean, that's true shit. You was with her home girl first, so hey, she can't say shit. Did you get that work?"

"Hell, yeah. What you think in this damn book bag? Some schoolbooks?" Tron unzipped the bag and pulled out a Ziploc bag full of powder bags.

"That's the lick right there."

Tron took a pull of the Kush. The potency caused him to cough a little. "We just need a few months to pump up and we can start our own shit. In the meantime, we gone flip this shit and keep copping work from Tori through Tweety, until we make it quadruple. Then after we start to take over, we eliminate the competition."

"I'm 'bout all that shit."

"Better be. You my right-hand, fuck you mean?"

"You fresh though." Jeff checked out the new Jordan's he was rocking with the matching 'fit. "I see you balled out with the cash I gave you."

Tron handed the blunt back to Jeff. "Nah. Tweety bought all this shit. I gave two grand of that money to Mya, so she could find us an apartment."

"Damn, you moving out already?"

"Nah. I just have to make sure my baby mama straight. She been out here doing it alone, with the help of Tweety. I'm home now, so I need to handle my responsibilities. Mya old girl kicked her out and she was staying with Tweety until I got out."

"Nigga, what? Tweety had her living there."

"Yeah, but check this though." He tapped Jeff on the arm, as he spoke with excitement in his voice. "The other day, Mya tells me she got kicked out on purpose so she could be close to me when I got home."

"Fuck, no!"

"G-shit, bro."

"So, all three of y'all living under one roof?"

"Yeah, but Mya haven't been staying overnight since I smashed her that night. She said she couldn't sleep under the same roof, knowing I'm fucking her and Tweety."

"Um, she knew that shit before she moved in."

"Shit, that don't matter. I fucked her in the house the other day when Tweety was gone."

"Damn, you a wild ass nigga."

"I know, but I can't help it. I fuck with Mya."

"Nothing wrong with that." Jeff turned the music up, allowing Plies to quake through the speakers.

Jeff drove them to Tron's mama's house and parked. When Tron saw Dazzle's car was outside, hopped out the car. "Oh, I'mma fuck this bitch up."

"Who, bro?"

"That bitch, Dazzle."

"Nah bro, chill."

"Fuck that." Tron rushed into the house and slammed the door behind him when he saw Dazzle sitting on the sofa. Her eyes widened in surprise and fear. She had no idea Tron was out. "Yeah, bitch, I'm home now."

"Boy, I don't give a fuck if you out."

Tron stood in front of her. "Why the fuck you kept my son away from me all those years?"

Dazzle rolled her eyes. "I don't owe you no explanation, so get the fuck out my face."

"And if I don't?"

"Tron, get out my face."

"Gimme some pussy. I know you missed me. Besides, you owe me for getting me sent to prison for all these years."

"I don't have time for this shit. Nor do I owe you shit." Dazzle picked up her keys and tried to get up, but Tron pushed her back down.

"Sitcho ass down."

"Tron, leave me alone, 'cause I'm not giving you shit. Go fuck Tweety or Mya." She tried to get up again, but he slapped her back down that time. *Whap!*

Dazzle swung on Tron and caught him in the face. Grabbing her hands, he pushed her down onto the sofa and straddled her. Repeatedly, he slapped her in the face. *Whap! Whap! Whap!* Dazzle screamed and tried to turn her head, so she could protect her face. "Tron, stop!" she screamed.

"I heard you out here fucking that nigga, Fresh. That's who you got my son calling daddy? Stupid ass bitch."

"He's more of a father than you ever been, bitch," Dazzle spat with so much hate in her tone.

"I'll show you a bitch." Tron used one of his hands to push her dress up to her waist and rip her panties on one side.

"Tron, stop. Don't do this, please."

"Shut up."

Dazzle squirmed to keep him from sliding in between her legs. Tears started to pour from her eyes. Out of all the things he did to her, this was the absolute worst. Heavy pounding against the door startled Dazzle, but she prayed whoever was on the opposite was coming to her rescue.

"Aye, Tron, open the door," Jeff yelled.

"Give me a few minutes, bro." Tron could see his shadow, as he walked back down the walkway. He looked back down at Dazzle and kissed her bloody bottom lip. "You made me hit you."

"No, I didn't. Get off of me. I hate you." Dazzle used her free hand to try and push him off of her.

"Stop saying stupid shit like that. I love you."

"No, the fuck you don't and even if you do, I don't care. I moved on long time ago."

"Fuck that nigga. You belong to me."

Dazzle spit in Tron's face. Her actions released a monster inside of him, and he used his left hand to choke her and his right hand to slap her up a few more times. Tron then took his right hand to pull his rock-hard piece out and plunged it deep inside her pussy. Dazzle clawed at his arms and neck to stop him, but it didn't help. He was too powerful. Realizing she lost the battle, she just laid there until he was done violating her body. The thought of him shooting his semen into her made Dazzle want to vomit. He was the last person on earth she wanted to fuck but there she was, getting raped by her son's father, right at his mother's house.

Finally, Tron was done. His face was sweaty and he was covered in scratches. He stood up and fixed his shorts. Extending his hand out, he tried to help her up. "Don't fuckin' touch me," she screamed.

Just as she pulled down her dress, the door opened. It was Sheila. Dazzle grabbed her purse and rushed towards the door. His mother immediately noticed the fresh tears covering her face.

"Dazzle, what's wrong?"

"Nothing."

Sheila didn't believe that for one second. "Tron, what the fuck did you do to this girl?"

"Nothing, Ma."

"Don't lie to me. Dazzle, tell me what happened."

Dazzle couldn't pull herself to repeat what had just occurred. So, she didn't answer her. "I'll pick up Jamir tomorrow." All she wanted was to go home and wash away every trace of him.

"Okay." Sheila looked back to Tron. "You hit her, didn't you?"

"No, Ma."

Sheila walked up to him and grabbed his face. She needed to look into his eyes. "Antron Davis, don't you lie to me. I saw the blood on her lip."

"Yes. I hit her a few times."

"Why?"

"Because she moved on and kept my son away from me."

"You can't be mad about that. You cheated on her more than once and had a damn baby. Not to mention, you with her ex-best friend. I swear, you act like I didn't raise you right at all. You just like your no-good ass daddy." Sheila pointed her finger in his face. "If she send the police over to lock your ass up, I'm not saying shit. I done told you about putting your hands on women, boy. You ain't gone be happy until one of their brothers or daddies kill your ass."

"I'm sorry, Ma."

"Yeah, I know that. Now, do better than this. Go outside and get your son. He in the backyard with Jeff." Sheila walked away, still ranting. "You acting like you miss prison already." Suddenly feeling bad, Tron went outside to find his son.

***

At the warehouse, Diesel stood at the head of the table with a mean mug and his pistol clutched in his hand. His camp was more divided than ever, and he needed to get it under control before the business suffered more than it already had. Byrd stood along the sideline with his hands folded, observing the reactions of the attendees.

"Lately, business has been steady, but we've been encountering problems left and right. Taking losses isn't something I'm used to and I'm not having any of that shit after today. If anyone has a problem with that, you might as well walk out that door right now."

The crew sat attentively, listening to their commander.

"The next thing I need to address is the chain of events that has led up to a few of our spots being invaded by some new competition. Does anyone know anything about that?"

An echo of no's rang out in the room.

"Well, allow me to fill you in on who's behind all of the chaos. It's my daughter, Tori. She's interfering in my business with a pack of wild, reckless niggas. I want this to be understood right here and now. If you ever cross paths with my daughter, which I highly doubt you will, do not touch her whatsoever. If I hear otherwise, I will torture and kill you. That's a promise. Now, if you run across any of her workers, feel free to light they asses up."

"So, your daughter is the reason my best friend dead?" Harold shook his head in disbelief. "I can't believe this shit."

"What's the problem?"

"I'm just saying, your daughter is the reason my nigga dead. This sounds like a family beef we getting pulled into."

"And what's your point?" Diesel spoke through gritted teeth.

"Nothing."

"Nah, speak on it, 'cause it sounds like you want out."

"It's not that, I just want the nigga who pulled the trigger. He gone pay for what he did." Harold was heated and hurt by the shit he just heard.

"And who gone get street justice for you?"

"What you mean?"

Diesel aimed his gun in Harold's direction and pulled the trigger. *Boc!* The bullet made a new home in his chest. Diesel then walked over to where Harold was sitting and gasping for air. Leaning forward, he looked directly into his face. "That sounded like a threat towards my daughter and you know I can't have that. Now you about to die for nothing." Diesel pushed the gun into his eye socket and pulled the trigger. *Boc!* Then he walked away as if he didn't just make a bloody mess.

"Okay. Does anyone else have a problem with the rule?" Diesel pointed his gun at every individual, as they stated *no* to his question.

# Chapter 14

Hurt was not the word that fit the way Dazzle was feeling. She felt betrayed and taken advantage of. Tron's foul mouth and many women had never destroyed her. It was the violation he committed against her body. In the car, she couldn't stop crying for nothing in the world. Her mind couldn't wrap around his reasoning for forcing her to participate in such a despicable act.

Dazzle was afraid to go home in the condition she was in. Her lip had a split in it and sex reeked from her pores. There was no way Fresh would understand what happened to her, and she didn't want him to feel as if she cheated on him. Then she thought about Tori or Lala, but she was far too embarrassed to admit she had been raped. After thinking about her next move, she picked her phone and called her man.

"Yeah, baby," Fresh answered on the second ring.

"Where are you?"

"On my way home. Where are you?"

"Same. Can you stop and get food please? I don't feel like cooking."

"What you want?"

"Surprise me. I'll be satisfied with whatever you get."

"I'll be home soon."

Dazzle felt relieved that she was able to buy some time and clean up before Fresh made it home. Driving like a bat out of hell, she zig-zagged throughout the afternoon traffic like her life depended on it. In reality, it did. Twenty-five minutes later, Dazzle pulled into her safe haven.

Quickly, she sprinted to the entrance and went inside. Dazzle grabbed a plastic bag from underneath the kitchen cabinet and placed her soiled, ripped panties inside. Once it was buried inside the trash can, she rushed to the shower like she had a fire underneath her ass. Making the water as hot as she could stand it, Dazzle stood in place as it beat against her skin. It was soothing, but it didn't dismiss the pain she felt deep down inside.

Closing her eyes didn't serve any justice. Tron's face, his scent and his touch invaded her mind vividly and played out like a horror-filled slideshow. Exhaling, she cried, as the water covered her face. It felt as if she was drowning, but her head remained in the same spot. Dazzle soaped up her washcloth and viciously scrubbed away every piece of DNA that Tron left behind.

The glass shower door slid open and Fresh stood there with an alluring smile on his face. "Showering without me, huh?"

Dazzle opened her eyes and observed her man standing there in the nude. As bad as she wanted to decline being touched, she couldn't pull herself to turn him down. Fresh didn't deserve to feel unwanted.

Feeling dirty all over, Dazzle closed her eyes and tried to push the negative thoughts out of her mind. Fresh lifted her by the waist and pinned her against the cold tile. Escaping the reality was what she needed, so she allowed her mind to drift off to someplace far away. In his arms, she always felt safe. There were no worries present after the day they met. Wrapping her arms around his neck, she relaxed and went with the flow.

When it was all over, Fresh was smiling with satisfaction, but not her. Dazzle felt worse than she did before. *How could she sleep with two men within one hour of each other? Should she confess?* Those were the questions that plagued her mind. Granted, it wasn't her fault, but it still felt like she cheated on the one and only man that ever loved her unconditionally.

After the intense, passionate shower, the couple retreated to the kitchen. The delicious aroma filled Dazzle's nostrils. "Baby, what did you get us?"

"Jamaican food."

"Oxtails." She smiled and rubbed her belly.

"You know it."

"I'm so hungry too." Dazzle was in desperate need of a drink. Opening the fridge, she pulled out the cold bottle of Cîroc.

"Fix me one too."

Placing his glass down in front of him, Dazzle sat beside him at the table. Quietly, they sat and indulged in their food. Dazzle kept stealing fast glances at Fresh with a painful, yet guilty expression on her face. The fourth time, he called her out on it.

"What's wrong, baby? Why you keep looking at me like that? Did I do something wrong?" Fresh sat his fork down and gave her his undivided attention. He knew he didn't do anything, but he wanted her to open up, just in case he missed something. As a young boy being raised by a single mother and a house full of women, Fresh knew how to communicate properly and effectively.

Dazzle reached across the table and grabbed his hand. "No baby. Never. Why would you think that?"

"I'm just asking, 'cause you keep giving me the side eye."

"It's not that. It's…" Dazzle's heart whispered, *tell him the truth*, but her mind screamed, *don't tell that man you just fucked the man he hates with a passion.* "Tron is out and—"

"You worried about that nigga?"

"No."

"You better not be. He ain't gone do shit to you. I'm here to protect you and our son." Over the years, Fresh and Jamir developed a father-son bond so strong, there was no one living and breathing that could tell him Jamir wasn't his child. Fresh took them as a package deal, and had been taking care of his family since day-one. And, would continue to do so with ease.

Dazzle wanted to admit he already did, but she kept quiet. Maybe things would blow over in time and she could forget about it all together. "Please."

"I got you, baby. I promise." Fresh pulled her hand in his direction and kissed it. "I'm not going to let him hurt you."

Dazzle got up and straddled his lap. "Just hold me." She always felt safe in his arms and right now, she needed him more than ever before.

\*\*\*

Tori sat in a rental car at the end of the street, looking at the picture of her and Kilo on their wedding day. She was dressed in all black. Her hair was pulled into a ponytail underneath one of Kilo's fitted caps. The photo was her reminder of what needed to be done. Using her pointer finger, she traced his face.

"I miss you so much, handsome. My world is fucked up behind this. You really fucked me up with this one. We need you bad out here, baby. I just need to see your face and hear your voice again."

The sound of screeching tires interrupted her talk with Kilo. When she looked up, the truck was headed up the block, so she pulled off right behind it. Picking up the burner phone she bought hours ago, she sent a text, *He's on the move.*

Tori followed the truck at a safe distance for the next twenty minutes, until they ended up on Cypress Creek. The occupant pulled into the gas station and got out. Making sure she was close enough, Tori backed into a parking spot facing the pump. Once he returned, he pumped the gas and watched his surroundings.

A black undercover squad car pulled up and parked directly on the side of it. Tori pulled out her cellphone and pressed record.

Stepping from the unit was a black man dressed in black slacks and a white dress shirt. He approached the vehicle with his hand on his holster. The two had a brief conversation, before the man was placed into the back of the car for approximately five minutes. Finally, the driver's door opened and the undercover opened the door for his prime suspect. Quickly, the man climbed back into the truck and pulled off. The undercover nodded in Tori's direction and went inside the gas station. Satisfied with the quick exchange, Tori stopped with the undercover work and went on her merry little way.

Tori pulled up into her quiet, secluded neighborhood, Heron Bay in Parkland. The security guard waved, as he watched her open the white metal gate with her key. Safety and security was what she looked for when it was time to move. In her line of business, she couldn't afford to let anyone know where she lived. Not even her girls. As far as they knew, Tori was living at the house with Eazy. Her decision to keep it a secret wasn't because she didn't trust them. It was solely based on keeping them safe as well. In the event there was an incident, they couldn't speak on what they didn't know. Nor could anyone follow them to her residence. One day, she would tell Lala and Dazzle, but for now this had to be something she kept to herself.

Tori's home was absolutely stunning. The two-story, four-bedroom, three bath home was approximately sixty-eight hundred feet and ran her six hundred thousand dollars. It was worth every penny spent. Hitting the clicker, she opened the two-car garage and pulled inside.

Once the door was closed, she climbed out and unlocked the side door. Tori smiled every time she walked into the living room area. Mounted on the wall was a painting of her and Kilo dressed in all white. The artist she hired did an amazing job at bringing her vision to life.

The kitchen was what she fell in love with more than anything. It had quartz countertops, wood cabinets, a huge cooking island, and stainless-steel appliances. LED lighting ran throughout the entire house. Her next favorite thing was the chandelier with an Aladdin lift system. Gray was the color scheme with a hint of purple. Perfect for taste and infatuation of royalty. After all, she was the queen. Tori looked at the diamond encrusted wall clock. She had six hours to rest before her date with Jude. Tired as hell, she sauntered into the kitchen and poured a glass of Patrón and lime juice. It had been a long morning and sleep was well needed.

Upstairs in her bedroom, Tori removed her clothing and took a quick five-minute shower. There was no such thing as climbing on clean sheets with a dirty body. Afterwards, she laid across the bed and drifted off into a deep, deep sleep.

Tori slept peacefully with a light snore. Darkness crept throughout the room and coldness caressed her spirit. The home was completely silently until heard a soft noise. Her eyes struggled to open, but the sleepiness was winning. "Mrs. Kingsley."

The sound of his voice rattled her spirit. When she rolled over, she saw him. "Baby, is that you?"

"Yes. It's me and I need to talk to you."

"About what?"

"I miss you so much and I never pictured life without you. But life happened. Diesel didn't want us together."

"Kilo, I love you so much. Why did you leave me here?" Fresh tears flowed from her eyes like a waterfall in Jamaica.

"I didn't have a choice, baby. But later for that. Listen to me carefully. I know all about Jude and no, I'm not mad with you for moving on. You've waited four years and you deserve to be happy. He's not a man of my caliber and you deserve better than that. Just keep your eyes on him. Also, what I need for you to do is to be careful, my love. Watch your surroundings and the ones closest to you. They don't mean you well. I'm sorry I'm not here for you and Capone, but not a day goes by that I don't think about the two of you. And believe me, I over-stand your reasoning for doing what you did."

"Kilo, I'm so sorry. I didn't want to do it, but I had no choice. Please don't be upset about that or Jude. He's just here to fill the equator-sized hole you left in my heart. I swear, I'll never love another man the way I love you."

"I know, baby. I've been watching you daily."

"Just come back to me. I'm going to die without you," she cried.

"You have to continue to live, Tori. Our love is eternal, and I'll be here with you forever. I promise."

"You promise?"

"I do. That's why I married you. I love you so much, Tori, and don't you ever forget that. Someday, we'll meet again." Kilo stood up to leave, revealing his all black attire. "Be safe and make sure you reign supreme. You are the true Queen of the Trap."

"Kilo, please don't leave me."

"I love you, Tori."

"I love you too, baby." She could feel his lips on hers, his hands on her body and slow strokes of passionate love. It was a feeling she never wanted to let go.

Two hours later, Tori woke up drenched in sweat on her body and face. Her wet eyes were sore to the touch. Rolling over, she grabbed her cellphone to check the time. It read 7:30 pm and Jude had called her three times. Dialing his number, she let the phone ring until he picked up.

"Yeah." There was slight irritation in his voice.

"I missed your calls. I'm just waking up."

"We still going out or you too tired?"

"Yeah. Give me an hour to get ready and be to your house."

"I can just pick you up," he insisted.

"No. I'll come to you. I don't feel too comfortable having you come to my father-in-law's house just yet. I won't take long."

"Okay. I'll be waiting."

After hanging up with Jude, Tori sat on her bed and recalled the conversation she had with Kilo. Honestly, it bothered her. However, she was a smart girl and could handle her own if the occasion arose. Kilo taught her well.

It took a good thirty-five minutes for her to slip on a pair of jeans, sexy top and a pair of heels. Happy with her appearance, she grabbed Kilo's gold Desert Eagle and left the house. While traveling southbound on the turnpike, she relived that moment with Kilo in her bedroom.

Tori sent Jude a text as soon as she made it to his complex. As she parked in the guest spot, she could see him approaching her vehicle. Jude opened the door. To her surprise, he had a smile on his face. "Hey, beautiful."

"Hey."

Tori stepped out the car, clutching her Desert Eagle. Jude shook his head and laughed. "Baby, we're going to dinner and a movie. Not Afghanistan. And I know you like what I'm packing instead."

Tori could do nothing but laugh at his humor. "Sometimes you should be paranoid. You never know who is out to get you."

"Yeah. You right about that, but you have me. I'll protect you at any cost."

"I appreciate that." Tori stood on her tippy toes and kissed his lips. "By the way, I'm leaving for Atlanta tomorrow."

"You need me to go with you?"

"No. I'm going with my brother-in-law. I'll be okay."

"What are you going for?"

"I have a place up there, so I need to go up and start packing my things. He's going to help me, since he lives there as well."

"You know you could've asked me to go with you. I would've went."

"It's okay. I'll be fine."

Jude sighed and rubbed his temple. "I get that, Tori, but as your man, you should've consulted with me first. I just don't feel comfortable with you being with another man and in another state at that."

Tori was completely blown by his reaction. She was a grown ass woman, and no one was going to tell her who she should be around, or where she should go. The man who contributed to her being on earth couldn't do that. Let alone a man she was dating.

"Jude, I think it would be best if I go home. Let's just cancel our date night."

Tori turned to walk away, but Jude snatched her by the arm and pulled her backwards. "No. We have plans."

"Jude, let me go." Forcefully, she pushed him away and released herself from him grip. "What's wrong with you?"

"Baby, I'm sorry. I'm just," he exhaled deeply. "Just come inside so we can talk, please."

"You need to go inside and relax. I'm leaving." Tori hit the remote and unlocked her doors before climbing in and securing the locks. Whatever he had going on was his problem, not hers, and she refused to fall victim to his hands. As she backed out of the guest spot, she could hear him calling her name.

Tori drove down Commercial in deep thought. First, Kilo came to her to send a warning and then Jude decided to reveal a jealous side to him. His actions were not sitting well with her at all. As she sat at the light, Tori caught a glimpse of a familiar truck at the Shell gas station. The man who stepped from the vehicle appeared to be someone involved in Kilo's murder. When the light turned green, she pulled into the gas station near the air pump and waited.

A few minutes later, Sherrod walked back to his truck and pumped the gas. It was evident someone was in the truck because he was having a conversation and smiling. Lying in wait, Tori sat with her foot on the brake until Sherrod pulled off.

Tori followed them to the light and busted a U-turn to get onto State Road 7. Trailing closely behind, Tori kept her hand on the Desert Eagle. The ride wasn't long at all. Sherrod quickly hooked a right into the Wellesley Inn Hotel and drove to the back of the building. Checking her surroundings, Tori parked several spots away from them and climbed out the car.

On the creep, she slid up to the driver's door and snatched it open. The woman in the passenger seat looked at Tori and snapped. "Sherrod, who the fuck is this bitch?"

Tori smirked. "Yeah, Sherrod, tell her who I am."

His mind was on the pistol he had on the floor. It was a long shot, but as soon as Tori was distracted, he was going to pull it out. "You cheating with this bitch?" The woman punched him in the arm.

"Baby, don't flatter yourself. I wouldn't fuck Sherrod with your pussy." Tori revealed her strap. "Sherrod, I think you know why I'm here."

The woman instantly started to hyperventilate. "What. What's going on?"

"Hoe, shut up." Tori kept her eyes on Sherrod. "Do you know why I'm here?"

"No." He shook his head.

"You killed Kilo."

Sherrod's expanded eyes were a dead giveaway. "Listen to me, it wasn't supposed to go down like that. It wasn't my fault, I swear."

"I'm listening."

"Diesel paid me to grab the nigga. When we got there, Kilo put up a fight and shot me. After that, Jarvis hit him, and we left."

Once she had the information she needed, Tori nodded and fired two head shots into Sherrod and his girl. *Boca! Boca!* Then she walked off into the dark night.

# Chapter 15

"Tweety!" AJ shouted as he ran into his stepmother's arms, giving her a big, heartfelt hug.

"Hey AJ. I missed you."

"I had fun with my grandma."

"You did?"

"Yep."

Tron dropped the baby bag on the couch and proceeded to leave the living room. Tweety quickly called out to him. "Baby, you okay?"

"I'm good." Tron was still upset about his run-in with Dazzle and wasn't in the mood to talk. So, he was hoping Tweety wasn't about to come in and twenty-question him to death. All he wanted to do was lay down and forget about the events from earlier that day. Little did he know that wish was about to be short-lived. Removing his shirt, he tossed it on the floor and kept on his wife beater.

While Tron twisted up a blunt using a Swisher Sweet, Tweety walked into the room with her hands on her hips. In silence she just stood there looking at him. He acted as if he didn't see her at first but another minute passed, and she was still there. Tron finally looked up at her.

"Why you just standing there like you a damn mannequin?"

"I'm just trying to see what's going on with you. I mean you did come in with an attitude, so it's easy to see that something is wrong."

"Why do you do that? I just told you I'm good. Leave it alone."

"Yeah, okay."

The last thing he wanted to do was argue at the place where he had to sleep, so he took a deep breath to calm himself down. "I'm just tired, baby, okay?" Tron lost the urge to smoke, so he sat the blunt in the ashtray on the side of the bed. "What AJ doing?"

"In the room watching *Hotel Transylvania*."

"He in the bed?"

"Yeah. I see he has on pajamas, so I didn't bathe him."

Tron laid back and rested his head against the soft pillow. "I gave him a bath at my old girl house."

"I figured that." Tweety sat down beside Tron. "So, did anything interesting happen today?"

"Nah."

Tweety ran her hand across his chest to keep him relaxed. "AJ told me he saw his brother today."

"He did." Tron's response was dry.

"Oh, where did he come from?"

Tron laughed out loud. "You think you so slick. That's what you was doing, questioning my son?"

Tweety was trying not to upset him. "No. He was telling me what he did over there and that he saw his brother. That's it. If I wanted to question someone, it would be you and not a child."

"Well, just say what's on your mind and stop beating around the damn bush. I know you like a book, so stop playing these childish ass games."

"Ain't nobody playing games with you, I'm just. Forget it," she huffed with aggravation in her slick tone.

"I already know where this is going, so let me end this shit now so I don't have to repeat myself. My baby mama dropped my son off to my mama house. Yes, I saw her and no she didn't know I was out. Old girl didn't tell her."

"That's it? Nothing happened?" Tweety was determined to get to the bottom of it all in order to clear up her insecurities. In her heart, she felt that Tron still loved her ex-best friend.

Tron opened his eyes to look at her. "Just ask me what you wanna know, 'cause you getting on my nerves with all this crazy shit." Tweety just stared at him in silence, unsure of how to proceed with her line of questioning. "What?" he shouted. "You wanna know if I fucked her? Well, I didn't. Damn, you trippin' already. If I would've known you was gone be on the bullshit, I would've came home to my old girl."

Suddenly, Tweety felt stupid and all her accusations did was cause tension in her home. This was not what she expected when her man came home after being gone for so long.

"I'm sorry. I just don't want to lose you. I'll stop, I promise."

Tweety slid her hands underneath his shirt, so she could caress his bare chest. Then she pulled the shirt over Tron's head, with his assistance. Seductively, she placed soft kisses on his chest and made her way up to his neck.

Licking on his spot, she ran across a rugged spot on the side of his neck. That caught Tweety by surprise, so she quickly examined the area. When she leaned back, Tweety noticed multiple scratches on his neck.

"Why the fuck do you have scratches on your neck?"

"What the fuck you talking about?"

Tweety screamed in his face. "You have scratches on your neck. Who you been fucking, Tron? And don't you lie to me either."

"Man, I ain't fuck nobody. You need to calm yo' ass down."

"You lying." Tweety's emotions began to take control of her and she swung on him with a closed fist, over and over again. "You out here fucking bitches who wasn't worried about your dumb ass when you was locked up."

Tron caught her hands as she tried to hit him again and rolled on top of her. His breathing was heavy and he didn't have the energy to fight with her. "I'm not about to fight you, 'cause I'll fuck around and kill yo' ass."

"Let me go now," she screamed.

"Not until you calm down." Tron waited until her body relaxed. Then he let her go. Without saying a word to her, he picked up his cellphone and dialed a number.

"What's up, bro? You good." Jeff asked.

"Nah. Come scoop me up and drop me off to my old girl house."

"Ah shit, what the hell happened?"

"I'll rap with you when you get here."

"Gimme thirty minutes and I'll be there."

"Yeah." Tron ended the call and put the phone into his pocket. He then grabbed a trash bag and placed some clothing in it.

"Where are you going, Tron?" Tweety grabbed his arm, but he snatched away from her grip.

"Get yo' fuckin' hands off of me. You know where I'm going. So, quit acting dumb." He continued to throw his personal items into a bag.

"You can't just pick up and leave whenever we have an argument."

"Watch me." Tweety kept trying to take his bag, but he continued to push her away. Finally, he stepped close to her face. "Now I can see why you was single before we met. You childish and insecure. Ain't no nigga in his right mind gone put up with this shit from you."

Tron listened to Tweety beg and plead for the next twenty minutes. Once he got the call that Jeff was downstairs, he took AJ from the bedroom and walked out the door, ignoring her cries.

***

**The next day**

**Atlanta, GA**

After an eight-hour drive, Tori and Honcho had finally arrived at their destination safely, when he brought the car to a stop in front of the apartments in Decatur.

Tori observed a group of dudes chilling in the parking lot, listening to music and drinking. "After we leave here, I need to shoot over to Villa Rica and drop off something to a friend of mine." She then checked the clip on her gun to make sure one was in the chamber, before tucking it away into her handbag.

Honcho put the car in park. "That's cool. We just need to handle this business first. Social calls last, sis."

Tori laughed. "This is business, bro."

"Okay. I'm just making sure you on point, that's all."

"Trust me, I'm not lacking."

"Good." Honcho popped the trunk and went to retrieve the knapsack. He and Tori then walked up on the porch. Honcho pounded on the iron door and waited.

"Who is it?" a male voice hollered from the opposite side of the door.

"Honcho, nigga."

The wooden door opened and there stood a tall, light-skinned dude built like a football player, with a huge grin on his face. He was very easy on the eyes, but not Tori's type.

"Houston, what it do, boy?" Honcho dapped his boy up, as he walked inside.

"Just coolin'. I'm glad to see you made it safely."

"No doubt. You know I know how to weave and elude them folks."

"That I do. Have a seat and get comfortable." Houston moved the soda cans and water bottles off the table to make the transaction smoother.

"Houston, this is Tori. Tori, this is Houston, my brother from another mother. One of the realist niggas I met on campus."

"Nice to meet you, beautiful. What you doing with this pretty ass nigga?" Tori couldn't resist laughing at Houston's humor.

"Well, if you must know, Tori is my sister. Better known as your boss."

Houston cleared his throat. "Damn, just like that, huh? You let me put my foot in my damn mouth." He then turned to Tori. "My apologies, boss lady. I didn't mean no disrespect."

"You good. I'm not easily offended."

"Whew!" Houston wiped his forehead as if he was sweating. "I ain't trying to cut off my supply chain before I get it."

"Sis definitely about her money, but she cool though." Honcho removed the pound of weed from his bag and sat in on the table. "This that real Florida Kush. These niggas gone be feenin' like crackheads for this shit. Watch what I tell you."

"As long as they got that cash, I don't give a fuck." Houston picked the bag and sniffed it. "That herb seeping through the bag. I know this shit hitting." He stood up with the package in his hand. "Let me grab this money real quick."

"A'ight." Honcho grabbed his vibrating phone from his pocket and opened up the text message. Chuckling, he replied and stuck it back in his pocket. "Lala wild as fuck."

"What happened?" Tori was curious as to what was being said.

"She talkin' about, don't be up here hittin' these thirst trap bitches or she gone fuck me up."

Tori shook her head, but she was not surprised at Lala's behavior. "I don't know what you did to my friend, but that girl gone. So, you better not be playing with her 'cause you know I can't jump in that."

"Damn, you supposed to be on my side."

"Nah, I love y'all the same and I'm not getting in the middle of that. Just keep it a bill with her and she'll be good. I promise you that. The worst thing you can do is lie to her."

"I'm not gone do that. I fuck with shorty the long way."

"I hope so."

"One thing about La, if you treat her good, she'll treat you better. My girl definitely a rider and will ride with you until the end, as long as she can trust you. Your word is all you have." Tori put him up on game, so he'll know how to move. The rest was up to him.

Houston walked in carrying a wad of money and passed it to Honcho. Quickly, he counted up twenty-five hundred dollars and tucked it away in his bag. "We gotta go, bro, and make some more moves. I'll try to slide back by here, but if not, I'll catch you on the next round."

"It's all good. I definitely understand." He hugged his boy and his new connect. "Nice to meet you, Tori. Hopefully, I'll be seeing you soon."

"Maybe." She smiled.

For the next two hours, Honcho and Tori slid through the north side of Atlanta, doing drop-offs and introductions to only a selected few of Honcho's most trusted friends. When the business was handled, they were finally free to relax.

"You ready to head out to Villa Rica?" Honcho glanced at Tori, who was gazing out the window. It appeared she was in deep thought since she didn't answer him. "Tori!"

"Yeah." She never took her eyes off the road.

"You still wanna go to Villa Rica?"

"Yeah." Tori pulled her phone out to make the call.

"Hello."

"Hey. I'm in town. Are you home?"

"Yes. We're here. Come on by," Professor Gordon happily replied.

"Okay. I'll be there in like forty-five minutes."

"We'll be waiting."

Tori could hear kids in the background laughing and playing. From the sound of it, they were having tons of fun. "See you soon."

The return to Atlanta was bittersweet, but it made her happy in so many ways. It was where she spent the last four years of her life. The place that turned her into a responsible woman. A small part of her wanted to come back to the Peach State, but the Sunshine State was her home. Like they say, home is where the heart is, but Georgia was where she planted her legacy.

Halfway up the street from her destination, Tori reached into the backseat and grabbed her large makeup bag. Inside was an envelope with twenty-five hundred dollars in it. She removed it and tucked it away in her purse, right beside her gun.

Honcho pulled up in the driveway. "You need me to get out?"

"No. I'm okay." She put her hand on the door and looked him in the eyes. "I'm going to be here for a while. Can you come back and pick me up?"

"Yeah. I got a homeboy who ain't too far from here. I'll go chill with him until you ready."

"Thanks. I'll hit you in a few hours."

"Okay."

Tori got out the car and closed the door. Taking slow steps up the walkway, she positioned her handbag into the crook of her arm and rang the doorbell. Professor Gordon answered the door and hugged her tight.

"Hey, beautiful. I'm glad you're back."

"It's good to be back." Tori turned back and waved at Honcho, as he drove away.

# Chapter 16

## U.S. Federal Building

## Ft. Lauderdale, FL

Lance showed his ID before gaining full access to the building. Taking the elevator to the third floor, he stepped off and proceeded to the third office on the right. Pushing the door open, he casually walked inside.

"We don't knock, do we?" Special Agent Smith leaned back in his leather chair.

"Since when have you known me to knock?" Lance made himself comfortable.

"You right," he grinned. "So, have you found out some valuable information?"

"Charro has just started to trust me and that's why I'm here. We just delivered a shipment here by boat and the transition was rather sweet."

"That means things are moving along quite nicely. A few more months and we can put a nail in his coffin." Special Agent Smith picked up a folder and slid it across the desk.

"What's this?"

"Domino. That's his Miami distributor. He was killed recently. There aren't many leads on the case, but that's not our main concern." Agent Smith folded his hands and placed them in his lap. "It's just a matter of time before he recruits a new one."

"And what do you mean, a few more months? Are you trying to get me killed?" Lance sighed. He became agitated quickly.

"If you do everything you're supposed to do, then you have nothing to worry about. Just don't blow your cover."

Lance's voice elevated, as he tried to get his point across. "I've been doing that, but you have yet to arrange a bust. This man is dangerous, and I'm outnumbered over there. I just told you we brought drugs over here by boat, in fruit boxes. He has the Coast

Guard on his payroll. As long as he has that, he won't have any trouble getting his dope over here."

"Well, if we stop it at the docks, it could be hard to prove they're involved. Be patient. The goal is to bring down the head of the organization. You ever heard the saying, 'kill the head and the body will die?'" Lance nodded his head. "That's what we have to do. Just be patient and all of this will be over soon. We need to build a case so solid that he doesn't stand a chance in the courtroom. We need direct evidence, not circumstantial if we want these charges to stick. Come on now, we've been doing this for four years, you know what to do."

"Got it. But you need to put in overtime. It's been eight months since we started this investigation and I'm just getting all the way in. That should tell you about the way he operates."

"Focus on getting me his entire pipeline. We can put the pressure on all of his distributors to testify in exchange for immunity."

"Yeah." Lance rose from his seat to leave.

"You wanna grab a drink since you're here?"

"I'm good. I have some business to handle before I head out of here tomorrow." Lance left the office feeling slightly defeated. If he wanted to bring his assignment to an end quickly, he needed to make a miracle happen. Not to mention he needed a plan to avoid the new distributor. Once again, he was putting his life on the line and quite frankly, he was tired.

\*\*\*

"I'm glad you decided to come over and spend the weekend with me." Mya stretched and placed her leg across Tron's waistline, while snuggling underneath him.

"I know you are." Tron rubbed the top of her head.

After the huge blowup with Tweety, he had Jeff drop him off to Mya's new apartment in Margate. She used the money to find a two-bedroom, through a private owner, who didn't hassle her too bad about being a teenage parent. The neighborhood was nice and quiet, exactly what Tron needed.

"Oh, really?"

"Yeah. I know you, so it ain't hard to figure out."

Mya had been contemplating on how to bring up the subject of him moving in, but she didn't know where to start. So, now was her chance since he opened that door slightly. "Well, if you know me so well, then why do you act like you don't know what I want from you?"

"I know you want me here with you and AJ, but…" Tron froze, trying to be careful with his words. He didn't want to move too fast and cause unnecessary problems between the women in his life.

Mya raised her head, so she could see his facial expression. "I'm listening. Don't stop."

"I have a lot of loose ends with Tweety that I need to tie up before I can leave her. It's complicated."

Mya rolled her neck. "It ain't more complicated than our situation, Tron, so stop it. You act like you have kids with her or something."

"I know that, but you not gone understand."

"You don't know that. You not even giving me the chance to not understand, because you not saying nothing."

Tron knew that if he didn't give her an explanation, she wouldn't let the issue rest. In order to keep her in place, he had to pacify his young love. "It's like this. Tweety put me on to her friend that supplies me dope. I need that connection and without her, I'll be cut off and I can't afford that right now. This is the only way I'll be able to pay for this apartment and take care of you and my son."

"Humph. I guess that means you ain't leaving her then. I knew you was gone pull this shit on me again." Mya's lip was poked out, as she whined like a child wanting a snack. "I'm so stupid to think you really wanted to be a family."

Tron exhaled heavily. It's not that he was aggravated. It was because the second chance his mother referred to was Mya. Sheila's words had been playing on repeat in his head since his first day out. One thing about Sheila, she had never led him wrong when it came down to advice. Therefore, he knew he needed to take heed to the lesson she was trying to teach him.

"Mya, stop."

"Why? Because I'm right and you know it. Just tell me you don't want to be with me now, so I can move the way I want to, and not worry about you and your situation." Mya was so pissed off she couldn't stand touching him at the moment. "You should've just left me alone. I was fine the way things were."

Tron's top lip curled. "What the fuck does that supposed mean? Move how you want to."

"Meaning you see who you want to, and I'll do the same."

"Girl, don't play with me. I never put my hands on you, but I will, if you try me." Tron's delivery with his words were clear enough for Mya to understand.

"And I'll tell your mama."

"I bet you would." Tron sat up and leaned against the headboard. "I'm going to say this one time, so listen carefully. There will not be a repeat of this conversation." Mya listened attentively until his phone started to ring. Tron looked over at the screen and saw it was Tweety, so he ignored it.

"Anyway, I want to be with you because I think this could work between us. But you have to be patient with me. All I need is a few months to get my weight up and I'll leave her."

Tron's phone rang again. He knew who it was, so he kept talking. "In the meantime, you have to chill out and not mess this up. So, before you decide to do pop-ups and start drama, just remember these bills have to be paid."

"A few months, Tron, really? Don't play with me."

"I'm not playing, ma, I'm serious. I wanna be here to help raise my son."

"Okay. I believe you." Mya straddled his lap just as his phone went off again. This time she grabbed it and powered it off. "You know she gone keep calling you."

"I know, but I don't feel like talking to her."

"Well, I turned it off."

Tron shrugged his shoulders. "Go close the door so I can get some, before AJ wake up."

\*\*\*

Tori woke up in the best of moods. Money was on her mind and she was ready to make one last move before their flight left out later on that night. Strutting out the bedroom, she walked into the living room of her apartment. Honcho was knocked out on the couch, snoring like a damn grizzly bear. Tori was cracking up, while she shook him. His eyes fluttered several times before he finally opened them.

"Damn, nigga, that's how you sleep?"

"What?"

"You was snoring loud as hell. I know Lala don't get no sleep unless she go to bed first."

Honcho sat up and stretched. "Shit, she louder than me."

"I know that's an awful sound in the mornings."

"Aye, that shit run in the family."

"That's a lie. Kilo never snored."

"I know you lying."

"I swear." That was the first time she said his name without having the urge to cry afterwards. "Our flight leaves at five-twenty, so we need to bust a move, because it's almost twelve."

"We just have the one meeting, right?"

"Yeah. After that, we can clear it."

"Cool. Go jump ya' ass in the shower. Because if I go first, you ain't gone like the smell of morning shit, while I smoke this Black & Mild."

"Oh my God, you act just like your bother. He did that shit every morning and I hated it. He used to get on my nerves, beating me in the bathroom. Now I miss that shit."

"I know you do. I miss that shit too," he agreed, while rubbing his hands across his sleepy eyes.

"Normally, I wouldn't allow smoking in here, but you can get a pass. Have ya' shitty ass ready when I get out." Tori went into the bathroom and hopped in the shower.

The weather in Atlanta was sunny, yet breezy. It wasn't cold. It was right in the middle. As usual, the traffic was congested as hell on I-75. Honcho lived there long enough to hit back streets and create shortcuts, so that wasn't a problem.

Finally, they made it to Mechanicsville, which was located in Zone 3. It was one of the rougher areas, but Tori didn't fear going to the hood. Besides, she had visited this same house on so many occasions, she'd lost count over the years. The home belonged to the cousin of Tori's college friend, Marcy. His house was the go-to spot when they wanted to be protected and party at the same time.

"Where you want me to park at?" Honcho asked, observing the yard full of cars.

"Just parallel park in front of the mailbox." From the road, she could see Chuck standing on the porch shirtless, exposing all of his prison tattoos.

"This house always crowded."

"How you know?"

"I done slid all up through here with my homies. I'm not as lame as you and my daddy think."

Tori picked up her bag off the floor. "I didn't say you were. Now pop the trunk, so we can get this over with."

The crew of men greeted Tori with hugs and dapped up Honcho. Chuck was standing there with his hair in messy braids. "Wussam, Tori. I see you missed the zone, shawty."

"You know I did." In the middle of their conversation, the group of men started shouting and making cat calls. When they turned around to see what was going on, they noticed a young girl walking up the street with little to nothing on.

"Don't call that nat nat over here," Chuck laughed. "Come on, let's go inside. Who you got with you?"

"This my brother, Honcho." After they greeted each other, they walked inside the house and sat down at the kitchen table.

Chuck remained standing with his arms folded. "How you plan on handling business? You moving back here or what? I need consistency."

"I'll be back and forth. But I can provide you with a consistent shipment. I still have my place here, so I'm rooted."

"That's good to hear, 'cause when I spoke with my cousin, she told me you hit it."

"I went back home to set up shop and lock in with my plug."

Chuck leaned against the wall. "So, how shit running down there?"

"Like a gold mine. My operation smooth as fuck and so is my team. I'm the queen down there," Tori boasted.

"Look at this shit here. Making moves like a boss." Chuck grinned and stroked his chin.

"This what I'm gone do. Gimme a key. I know that ain't a lot, but I have to make sure this shit potent. It's just business. My patna nem gone push this shit and see how they like it. If it's what you say it is, then I'm gone grab five when you come back. Once I pump up, I'll double, maybe triple the load. I'll throw in an extra stack for every key delivered."

"That'll work." She agreed to his terms.

"I'm gone make you a rich woman. Just wait and see."

"That's what I want to hear."

Chuck snapped his fingers. "Oh yeah, my brother in Tennessee looking for a new plug too. He waiting on me to give him the green light on this product. As long as everything good, I'll give you an introduction and you can be his supplier."

Tori smiled. That was music to her ears. With distributors in different states, there was no doubt she was about to be a Queen Pin.

After discussing numbers and kicking it for old time's sake, Tori and Honcho left at three so they could return the rental and be on time to catch their flight.

"I must say, this was a good ass trip. What you gone do about that money? You have a lock on that small suitcase?" There was a lot of concern in his voice.

"It's ten grand, so we good. Next time, we can't catch a flight. We'll have too much money. I'll have everything in order by the time we return. We can't afford to get caught up on the house. Now, you might have to come back with Lala. I'm sure she won't mind taking this trip with you."

"You know she ain't gone mind. That gives her a chance to watch my ass," he joked.

"Get off my girl. You know she fucked up about you."

"Yeah, she showing me that."

The check in at the Hartsfield-Atlanta Airport was smoother than expected. Normally, the extremely large airport was hectic and stressful. After a successful trip, Tori slept peacefully throughout the flight. Occasionally she would smile in her sleep, as she had sweet dreams of living a normal life, being a mother and a wife, again.

# Chapter 17

### Bianca's Hair Boutique

Monday rolled around quickly and Tori was not ready to start her day too early. She just needed a little more sleep. Instead of going in at ten, she had Lala go and open the store. When noon hit, she was walking through the doors and as usual, the store was packed. That was the plus to opening a beauty supply store in the hood.

One of her associates was at the register cashing out a customer. She looked up and smiled. "Hey, Miss Tori."

"Hey, Kesha." She smiled back. "Where is Lala and Shay?"

"Lala in the back and Shay come in at one."

"Okay."

Tori walked into the small office in the back. The door was ajar, so she walked right in and spotted Lala sitting at the desk with a bouquet of long-stemmed red roses in a crystal vase. "Hey, sis. Where you get flowers from?" Lala was so tuned into her phone that she didn't hear Tori enter the office. "Lala!" she shouted.

Startled by the voice that caught her off guard, she placed her hand over her heart. "You scared me, girl."

"What you looking at?"

"Look." Lala passed the phone to Tori. Her hands trembled hard and fast. "We going to prison."

Tori watched as the news reporter talked about the murder and how they didn't have any suspects in custody or any leads in the case. She handed Lala back the phone. "They don't have any leads, just relax. This will all blow over sooner or later."

"I hope so, 'cause I'm too pretty to go to jail. And it ain't no dick in there." Lala attempted to make light of the situation to keep from panicking.

"You not going, but you need to get rid of your phone. Turn it off and take out the SIM card."

"I had this number forever."

"Well, keep it and go to jail. Simple."

"Fine." Lala removed the SIM card from the phone and sat it on the desk. "You gone get rid of it for me?"

"Burn it out back."

"Okay." Lala rolled backwards in the chair and stood up. "Your man sent you some flowers I see, and a gift." She picked up the box and shook it. "Sounds like jewelry."

"Jude been here?"

"No. The delivery man dropped it off." Lala passed her the box. "Open it so I can see what's in it."

"I'd rather not."

"Why? You mad at him?"

"You can say that."

"Bitch, what happened?"

"He got upset when I told him he couldn't go with me to Atlanta and that Honcho was going with me." Tori walked behind the desk and sat down. "Talking about he don't feel comfortable with me being out of town with him."

"Oh, he must don't know you and Honcho really like sister and brother. That nigga wildin' if he think y'all gone fuck."

"He stupid as fuck if he think that."

"I agree. He can't possibly know you, if he feel like that."

"My point exactly. I haven't even called him since I been back. He been calling, but I haven't answered none of his calls." Tori was slightly frustrated, but she wasn't about to let that affect her day. "I don't know. I'm starting to think messing with him was a mistake. Like, I should've took more time to myself."

Lala sat on the edge of the desk with her hand on her knee. "I mean, you have to move on one day, so don't feel bad for making that effort. You've grieved long enough."

"Have I really?" Tori looked at Lala for approval.

"Yes. You have." Lala placed her hand on top of Tori's hand. "You've been through a lot and honestly, you stronger than most of us. I don't think I would've accomplished shit if I was in your shoes."

"Thanks. It's just hard to not think about the what ifs, you know. This is the most difficult thing to deal with in life. I wouldn't wish this on my worst enemy."

"There's no time limit on grief. What you and Kilo had was real love. History. That's hard to get over. Take all the time you need and don't allow anyone to make you move faster than you need to. Not even Jude."

Tori giggled. "Look at me taking advice from you. That's normally my job."

"Hey, a bitch is good for something. I'm not here just to look pretty and shit."

"That's good to know."

"Yeah, appreciate a bitch like me." Lala hugged Tori tight. Like it would be her last time doing so. "I love you so much, T, and I'll be here with you through it all. I swear I am."

"I appreciate that so much. You just don't know. Real friends are so hard to come across."

Lala released Tori quick and grabbed her shoulders. "Bitch, are you serious? I will do a bid for you. Don't play with me."

"No, the hell you won't. I need you to stay free for me. What am I supposed to do without you? Me and you closer than Dazzle and Tweety when we rocked like that."

"You right about that."

"Thank you. Now chill out with that prison talk. We gone be good, ain't nobody going to jail." Tori smiled at Lala. "Now get out of here. You have a lot to do and cover up. Hit me up later."

"I'll do just that."

"I love you, sis."

"I love you too." Lala turned on her heels to leave, but before she could get far Tori called out to her.

"Close the door please."

Lala was in the middle of the hallway when she stopped and turned around. Peeking inside, she laughed. "You better be lucky I was close, heffa." Lala left the office feeling confident the entire ordeal would blow over.

Tori signed onto her computer to go over the inventory and sales. Just then, a knock on the door interrupted her task. Slowly it opened, but she never took her eyes off the computer. "I thought you had shit to do. Why are you back?"

"I can't stay away from you."

To her surprise, it wasn't Lala. Instead, it was Jude. That was the last face she expected to see. There wasn't a single smile present. Jude peeped her unpleasant demeanor off top.

"Damn, don't look too happy to see me."

"I'm not." Tori looked away and focused on her computer screen to ignore her unwanted guest.

"Baby." Jude approached her desk cautiously. "I'm sorry. I know you're mad at me, but please give me a chance to explain my actions."

Tori placed her elbows on the table and folded her hands underneath her chin. The way he acted had her heated and she couldn't wait to put him in his place. She took a deep breath before setting the record straight.

"Jude, honestly, you don't owe me an explanation. I saw what I needed to see from you. You exposed your insecurity and I don't like that. Also, I feel like you tried me as if I would sleep with my brother-in-law. That told me exactly what you see when you look at me. And for the record, I don't get down like that, in case you missed the memo. I'm twenty-three years old and you are the only man that had the luxury of sleeping with me since Kilo died."

Tori's words felt like a kick to the stomach. She spared no expense when it came to crushing his feelings and male ego. Jude stepped in front of her and grabbed her hand. "Tori, I swear I don't see you like that. You're a good girl and I know this."

Tori snatched her hand away from him, crushing him even more. The touch of his hand made her cringe. Jealousy wasn't something she was used to. "I can't tell."

The feelings he started to have for her wouldn't allow him to walk away easily. Jude needed to plead his case and win her back by any means necessary. "Just listen to me, please."

Tori nodded and gave him the attention he asked for.

"Unlike you, I haven't had the luxury of having a fairytale relationship. The last woman I gave my heart to, shitted on me. She cheated on me and not only that, she did it in our bed." Jude got down on his knees and grabbed her hands again. This time, she didn't pull away. "That really fucked me up, but at the same time, I can't make you pay for her mistake."

Tori sat in silence as she listened to him admit his faults and explain his bad relationships for the next hour. A part of her felt bad for him, but on the other hand, that excuse didn't seem valid enough to take him back. However, she understood his pain. Not from personal experience, but what she witnessed firsthand with Dazzle. Jude looked in her eyes and he could see the lack of emotion in her eyes. It was obvious she wasn't trying to forgive him.

"I'm begging you, Tori. Please give me one more chance. I promise you won't regret it."

Tori shook her head. "I don't know about that. Something is telling me this is not going to work."

"Why you think that?"

"I'm in the dope game. I deal with men on a daily basis. How can I operate a successful business, surrounded by men, if you are insecure about your position in my life? That won't work."

"I'm telling you, it won't happen again. You've never given me a reason to not trust you and you didn't deserve that."

"All of that sounds good, but actions speak louder than words."

"I'll show you. Just give me one last chance. I'm begging you. We can start with lunch."

Tori was a little flattered, but that didn't mean he was back in her good graces. "Fine. I'll go."

"I promise you won't regret this." Jude stood up and placed a kissed on her soft, glistening lips. "Can you open my gift now?"

"In a few." Tori picked up her phone and sent Lala a text. Gathering her things, she shut off her computer and stood up. "I'm ready now."

# Chapter 18

Lala rolled over to see who had just sent her a text. The screen displayed Tori's name with the message, *I'm leaving the store with Jude. He came by to apologize in person and take me to lunch.*

She quickly responded, *Okay. I'll check on you later.* After leaving the shop, she passed a local lake and decided to toss the phone. The SIM card remained in her wallet for safekeeping. In need of a guaranteed stress reliever when her task was complete, Lala paid her lover a visit at his father's house.

Honcho walked out the bathroom wearing absolutely nothing. Lala licked her lips, as she scanned over his muscular physique and nice package. "You definitely know how to please a girl."

"That's my mission. To keep you wanting more." Honcho climbed back in bed and pulled the blanket over his body.

"Well, it's working like a charm."

Honcho laid on his side with his head propped up on the pillow, so he could bask in her flawless beauty. "You sure about that?"

"Yes. I'm sure."

"Don't play with me. I hate to fuck yo' chocolate ass up."

Lala was blushing hard. To hear Honcho stake claim was cute in her eyes. "No, don't you play with me. You the one who live in another state. I know you messing with someone up there."

"Man, you crazy. I be chillin'."

"I'm being serious."

"I am too," Honcho truthfully spoke.

"So, nobody occupying your time?"

"Yeah."

Hearing those words prepared her to snap. "Who?"

"You," he chuckled.

"That's funny, huh?"

Honcho pinched her cheek. "You should've just saw your face."

"That shit ain't funny."

"On the real though. I was messing with this chick, but I ended it. My interest lied elsewhere once I figured out what I wanted."

"And what do you want?"

With a straight face, he gazed into her eyes and pushed her hair from her face. "I think we should try this again. Ever since we linked back up, these old feelings returned and I know you feel the same way. It's more to us than just sex. I want something solid. The same love that Kilo and Tori had."

Lala was surprised he was speaking on some grown man shit. Whoever had been getting into his head did a great job at opening his eyes to see a bigger picture. It was something she wanted, but too afraid to admit it on her own. Out of fear that he didn't want the same thing. Now was her chance since she knew how he was truly feeling.

"I want to be with you too. I've felt like this for a while now, but I never said anything because I didn't think you felt the same way."

"Why? We have history and a good friendship."

"Honestly, I was scared to take that chance. With you being in Atlanta and I'm here, there was no way that was going to work. I know you deal with other females up there. I'm not crazy."

"That's in the past. I'm here with you trying to make things official. Listen, I don't have anything to hide. And to prove that to you, when I make this trip back up there, you can go with me. Are you down with that?"

"Yep," Lala didn't hesitate to respond.

"You know I'll be trafficking across state lines. You sure you want to come?"

"I'm riding with you on every trip."

"A'ight now, we leaving in a week."

"Oh, don't you worry, sir, my bags will be packed."

Lala was excited about rekindling things with Honcho and making it official. Leaning forward with her lips poked out, he met her halfway for a lip lock. Honcho rolled on top of her and kissed her all over the chocolate skin that he loved since the day they met.

"You ready for round two?"

"I stay ready." She smiled.

\*\*\*

**Margate, FL**

"You leaving?" Mya questioned, as she watched the father of her child get dressed.

"Yeah. I have an early day tomorrow and you have school."

"Well, who gone watch him if you running errands?" Mya sipped on a Fanta strawberry soda, while waiting on a response.

"I'll probably just take him to my mama house. I already know what I'm about to walk into when I get home." Tron leaned down and put on his shoes.

"See, that's why you need to move in here with me and we wouldn't have to worry about any of this." Mya sat her soda down on the side of the bed and crawled up behind Tron. Wrapping her arms around him, she kissed his neck. "We can be together every single day and night. Don't you want to wake up to me and your son?"

Tron knew that conversation was going to arise when it was time for him to depart from the residence. He understood her issue with the situation, but she had to be patient. There were too many loose ends to just up and leave like that.

After lacing up his kicks, he grabbed ahold of her hands. "I do and I told you that already. But you have to give me time to get everything in order. I'm about to get this car and my license in a few weeks. We can't maneuver without transportation."

Mya sighed and let him go. "Fine. I get it."

Tron turned around to face Mya. Her face displayed sadness and she refused to give him eye contact. "Don't start that. I've been here for days. You knew I had to leave eventually."

"Alright. Bye."

"I done told you what the deal is. So, quit making shit difficult." Tron walked to the opposite side of the bed and placed his hand on her face. Slightly, he turned it in his direction. "You love me?"

"You know the answer to that question already." Mya was slowly becoming an emotional mess. Therefore, it took no effort for her to drop a few tears.

Tron huffed with slight aggravation present and wiped her eyes. "What you crying for?" Mya shrugged her shoulders. "You acting like a nigga never coming back, or like I don't wanna be with you or some shit."

Mya sniffled and wiped her face on her shirt. "I just don't want you to leave."

"I'm coming back. I promise. Now tell me you love me."

"I love you." Mya didn't hesitate to make her feelings known.

Tron pop-kissed her lips. "Love you too, BM. I'll talk to you later."

"Okay." She nodded her head slowly with pouty lips and a pitiful stare.

"Where's my key?"

"In the top drawer."

Tron removed the key and slipped it onto his ring. "Don't have nobody in here while I'm gone. I will be poppin' up unannounced."

"I'm sure you will. AJ, come here." The boisterous toddler beelined into the bedroom with a bright smile on his face. It made Mya smile. Keeping her baby was the best decision she made in life. "Come give Mommy a hug."

Mya took pride in being a mother. When AJ entered the world, he forced her to grow up and become a responsible young adult. She hugged her little man tight and kissed his cheek. "Mommy loves you so much."

"I love you, Mommy." AJ gaped into her eyes and put his tiny hand on her face. "Don't cry, Mommy. We'll be back." He then focused his attention up at Tron. "Right, Daddy?"

"That's right, man. Let her know."

Tron's phone went off. He looked at it and pushed it back down in his pocket. "We gotta go, baby. Jeff outside waiting on us."

Mya watched the only two men she loved walk out the room. Once she heard the door close, she laid down and wrapped herself up in a blanket. The scent of Tron's cologne lingered on the pillow beside her. Instantly, she missed him. Grabbing the pillow, she snuggled up with it. Holding onto his scent was necessary, since she had to sleep alone. That was her reminder that their situation was only temporary.

\*\*\*

Tweety sat on the sofa drinking vodka with pineapple juice and watching re-runs of *Martin* in an angry slump. Tron had the nerve to be MIA for days and ignore every last one of her calls. Livid wasn't the word. She wanted to kick his ass for disrespecting her.

Rocking back and forth, she mumbled to herself, "I'm gone fuck his ass up whenever he walk through this door. He got me fucked up, if he think he gone try me like this."

Tweety took another sip, further drowning herself into a drunken state. Then she picked up her phone. Scrolling through her call log, she dialed Tron's number again. This time, it rang several times before going to the voicemail.

Her mind couldn't grasp the fact that he was beginning to treat her the same way he treated Dazzle. As she continued to scroll through the log, she opted on sending a text in hopes of getting to the bottom of things.

*Tweety: Hey. How are you and AJ?*
*Mya: We're good. U?*
*Tweety: I'm good. Have you seen Tron?*
*Mya: Not since I picked up the baby a few days ago*
*Tweety: Okay*
*Mya: Is he okay?*
*Tweety: Yeah. I'll talk to you later. Thanks*
*Mya: Yw*

Tweety threw the phone onto the sofa. The sound of the door unlocking was satisfying. It had been the moment she was waiting on. She downed the remainder of her drink and waited on him to enter. Tron crossed the threshold and locked the door behind him. To her surprise, he was alone. He looked at her and didn't open his mouth. Tweety was full of anger as she jumped to her feet.

"You just gone walk yo' ass in here and not say anything to me after being gone for days?" Her finger was now in his face. "You better answer me."

Tron stepped back and took a deep breath. "Tweety, get yo' fuckin' hand out my face."

"And if I don't?" She continued to antagonize him.

"Man, gone before I slap the shit out of you." Tron pushed her hand out his face and attempted to walk away, but Tweety grabbed his arm forcefully.

"Don't walk away from me."

"Girl, get your hands off me." Tron gave Tweety a hard push. He sent her flying into the edge of the sofa.

Tweety was furious. Back on her feet, she ran towards him and pushed him from behind. Tron's body slammed against the edge of the bedroom door. When he turned around, there was darkness in his eyes. Tweety ignored his evil stare and slapped him across the cheek with an open palm. Then she balled up her fist and threw wild punches against his frame.

"You out here running around with these nothing ass hoes and not coming home at night. None of them bitches was there for you during your bid, you dumb ass nigga," she frantically shouted.

Tron ducked and dodged a few of the punches, until he was finally able to restrain her. Grabbing Tweety by the wrists, he slammed her against the wall and pressed his arm against her throat. Tweety tried her best to get free so she could catch her breath.

"Let me go," she gasped.

Tron knew Tweety wasn't going to stop, so he kept the pressure on until she began to relax. Once he let go, Tweety struck him in the face. Tired of the irrational behavior, Tron needed to show her that he ran their relationship. Knocking her to the floor, he stood over Tweety and punched her repeatedly in the ribs and a few times in the face.

"This what you want? You want me to beat your ass?" He continued to pummel her with his fists.

"Nooo!" Tweety screamed, while covering her face from the vicious blows.

"I told you to stop. You wanna see how bad shit can get? I'll show yo' muthafuckin' ass," he spat angrily.

Tron grabbed his woman by the hair and dragged her into the room. Tweety kicked and scratched, as her body slid with ease across the cold, tiled floor. Loud agonizing screams filled the room, but that didn't stop the beating. In fact, it intensified. Tweety began to see stars. Curling up in the fetal position, she prayed for the torture to come to an end. Tron kicked Tweety in her side until she stopped fighting. Stretched out on the floor, she laid there bloody until he left the room and closed the door. Tron sat in the living room and rolled a blunt to calm his nerves. The last thing he wanted to do was beat her ass, but Tweety forced his hand. Therefore, she had to suffer.

Tweety struggled to get up. The tenderness of her stomach made it difficult. Every inch of her body ached. Grabbing the footboard, she managed to get on her feet. Slowly, she stepped towards the mirror to see the damage. She could taste the fresh blood inside her mouth, but she was too afraid to touch her swollen lip. Tweety sobbed the moment she laid eyes on her battered and bruised face. There was no doubt she was about to rock two black eyes. In need of her phone, she stumbled out into the living room. Tron was relaxing as if he did nothing wrong.

Picking up her phone, she looked him in the eyes. "Do you see what you did to my face? I hope you're happy."

When Tron didn't acknowledge her, she went back into the room and laid down. But not before she took pictures of the bruises she sustained at his abusive hands. For the first time since the two had been together, she felt Dazzle's pain.

After an hour of silent cries, Tweety was finally able to doze off into a light sleep. Fear shook her to the core when she felt the bed move. Tron placed his hand on her back and she trembled. Afraid of what he would do next, she remained still.

"Baby, you sleep?"

Tron put his arm around her and stared at the awful handy work he left behind. "Damn," he sighed. "I fucked up." Suddenly, he felt bad for his aggressiveness towards her. Gently, he kissed her forehead. "I'm sorry." Then he cuddled up beside her until he fell asleep.

# Chapter 19

## One week later

## Memphis, TN

Honcho thumped on the lodging entryway of room 316 and waited on an answer. Standing at his side was his lady luck, Lala. She was more than happy to make the fourteen-hour drive with her man. Seconds later, a single click could be heard, before the door became ajar. In the frame stood a husky, medium-built man. He was bald, with a tattoo of a skull on his head. The bodyguard eyed the new faces.

"Honcho?" he questioned.

"Yeah. I'm here to see Todd."

"Come in." Husky dude stepped to the side, allowing them to enter.

Upon entering the room, Todd was sitting down on the sofa observing his new supplier. From the disarray of the room, it was obvious that a party took place. There were liquor bottles scattered all over the counter. Cigar wrappers and weed residue were on the table.

Honcho instantly noticed the strong resemblance between him and his brother, Chuck. Todd rose to his feet. "It's good to finally meet you, Honcho."

Both men shook hands.

"Todd, this my lady."

"Nice to meet you." Todd greeted the lady of the hour.

"Same here." Lala smiled and rubbed her baby bump in a circular motion.

Todd pointed to the empty spot on the sofa. "Have a seat. You shouldn't be standing on your feet like that."

"Thanks." She smiled pleasantly.

Lala took a load off and sat patiently, yet attentive, while Honcho conducted business. The guard was giving off this funny vibe. He kept moving around like he couldn't keep still. That put Lala on high alert. Slowly, she folded her arms across her belly and stuck her right hand inside her jacket. Lala was carrying a small Glock, so she was able to grip it without a problem. With her finger slightly on the trigger, she waited.

"You want a drink?" Todd pointed towards the liquor bottle on the table.

"Nah. I'm good. Let's handle this business." Honcho sat the duffle bag on the table and counted the kilos one by one, until he reached twenty-five.

"All work, no play, huh," he joked.

"That's all I know."

Todd used a knife to slit open the package. Using his pinky, he dipped it inside and covered his finger with the snow-white product. He then rubbed the product across his gums. In need of another sample, he scooped a nail-sized amount and snorted it.

"Yeah," he grunted. "That's that good shit." Todd followed the same procedure on the second package. Satisfied with his new product, he looked at his partner and nodded his head. "Aye, P, grab that cash for me and that money counter."

Everyone sat in silence. The only noise that could be heard was the sound of the money running through the counter. After a smooth transaction, Honcho and Lala left the room and loaded the money into the trunk of the car.

On their way back to the Big Cypress Lounge, they stopped for food and continued their journey. Honcho glanced over at Lala. "So, how was your experience?"

"It was cool. The bodyguard seemed strange, that's why I kept my arms folded."

Honcho laughed. "You had your finger on the trigger?"

"Hell, yeah. I don't know them niggas."

"You'll shoot a nigga about me, huh?"

Lala reached over and grabbed his right hand. "I would've aired that muthafucka out."

"That's what I'm talking about." Honcho kissed her hand. "I'll do the same for you."

"You better."

The blaring sound of sirens interrupted the love birds. Honcho glanced in the rearview mirror. "Shit, they pulling us over. Put on your seatbelt," he instructed, while doing the same thing.

There was a shopping plaza on the right, so he pulled in where other patrons could be seen out in the open. Before the officer made it to the car, Honcho rolled down the window. The cop walked up and looked inside the vehicle.

"Good afternoon, license and registration please."

"Sure thing, but can you tell me why you pulled me over?"

"Just a routine traffic stop. We do that often here whenever we see a Florida tag."

"Racial profiling, I see." Honcho shook his head. "I'm just bringing my wife on a trip before the baby gets here."

"There has been a lot of fraudulent activity and we're just trying to keep a handle on it. It's not a race thing, sir."

Lala reached inside the glovebox and pulled out the rental car agreement. "Here. I'm tired and I want to lay down." Lala rubbed her stomach again. "I don't feel too good."

"As long as your license is valid, you can leave."

Honcho removed his wallet from the middle console, took out his license and passed it to the officer. "Here you go."

The officer looked at the photo, then back to Honcho. "You're free to go. Take your wife back to the hotel so she could get some rest."

"Thank you." Honcho retrieved his items back and handed them to Lala. Then they pulled off.

"I told you my fake baby bump would pay off."

"Yeah, you did."

\*\*\*

Dazzle woke up early in the morning and got dressed. She had a delivery to make. In addition to that, Jamir needed to be dropped off to camp. Normally, Fresh would do it, but he had errands to run with his mother that day. "Jamir, let's go. We gone be late."

"I don't want to go to camp. Can I just stay home?" he pouted.

"You can't. Fresh not gone be here."

Fresh walked into the living room brushing his hair. "What's going on out here?"

"He don't want to go to camp," Dazzle replied.

"Jamir, why you don't wanna go to camp?"

"I don't like them kids. Can I stay with you, please?" he begged.

Fresh chuckled. "You can stay. Go ahead, baby. I'll just take him with me."

"Are you sure?" she double checked, knowing full well Fresh had trouble telling him no.

"We good. Go handle your business."

"Okay. See y'all later."

Dazzle kissed the men in her life before rushing out the door. It was slightly humid outside. The wind wasn't blowing at all. "Whew, this is bathing suit weather."

Cruising through the streets, she made a few turns and so did the car behind her. Almost certain she was being followed, she stopped using the turning signal and made a sharp left. The car was still behind her.

"Who the fuck is this?" she mumbled.

On her way out the neighborhood, Dazzle turned onto 56th Avenue and headed northbound to blend with the other cars. The drive lasted a half of a mile before she heard the sound of a siren going off.

Dead on the spot, she started to panic. "Fuck!"

With no other options on the table, Dazzle pulled over into the parking lot of the hotel and put it in park. "Whew! Whew! Okay. Calm down. Everything will be okay." Dazzle's breathing was rapid, yet quick, like she was having contractions.

Glancing over her shoulder, she could see a well-dressed, middle-aged black man approaching the vehicle with shades on. He tapped on the window with his knuckles. Dazzle took a deep breath before she rolled it down.

"How can I help you?" she gave him a tremulous smile.

Flashing his badge, he replied, "I'm Detective Terrell Andrews."

"Detective?" His title caught her off guard. "Is it common for detectives to pull citizens over?"

"Of course it is, Travonda Sutton," he whistled, while calling out her government name.

Now Dazzle was really nervous, but she did her best to remain calm. It was hard not to let him see her sweat. "How do you know my name and what do you want?"

"Well, you are a person of interest in the death of Terry Andrews."

"Who?" She scrunched up her face.

"Terry Andrews. You were at his house, correct?"

"I'm sorry, but I don't know what you're talking about," she lied. Dazzle knew exactly who he was referring to, but there was no way she would admit to it.

"Listen, don't play games with me. I know you were there because I saw the fuckin' video. Now, who were you with?"

If it wasn't for Lala putting her up on game of the bad video, she probably would've cracked on the spot. "You have the wrong person."

"Well, tell me this. Who is Laneisha Huntley?"

"Sir, I don't know." Once again, she lied. That time it was about not knowing Lala's government name. In her mind, she thought, *this nigga knows an awful lot.*

Terrell was growing irritated with his suspect. He spent more than enough time investigating this case off the books to know she was lying. However, he had no proof and without admittance to any of the questions he'd asked, there was no way he could arrest her. The seasoned detective knew he had to push further.

Pushing the rim of his shades up, he leaned closer into the window. "See, what I can't stand is a fuckin' liar. But you know what I'm going to do for you? I'm going to let you in on a few details. What you don't know is that I've been following you around since his murder. I've watched you with the woman, whose phone number was located in the phone. So, you can continue to lie, but the truth is going to come out and when it does, I'm going to make sure you get the death penalty for such a horrific and heinous crime."

Dazzle sat there stuck, frozen in time, as she listened to his recent activities. "Can I go now?"

"With me? Of course you can. You can go with me willingly, or by force. And if you choose force, I can guarantee little Jamir will never see his mother again. Not even in prison. After they lay you to rest, he'll only be able to visit you with flowers."

Dazzle was completely shaken up. Nor did she know what to do. Detective Andrews was at his wits' end with her, so he pulled his weapon from his holster. "Get out of the car. Now!" he screamed.

Doing as she was told, Dazzle opened the door and got out.

"Now put your hands behind your back." She followed every instruction. Once she was cuffed, he placed her in the backseat of his cruiser.

Dazzle watched as Detective Andrews searched her car. Those actions gave her an immediate heart attack. "Fuck! The dope." She mumbled under her breath, while rocking in the seat.

The detective moved swiftly to his car and climbed inside. In his right hand, he held up the kilo of cocaine. "You know what this is?" he laughed. "Of course you do. This right here is going to guarantee you a life sentence."

"No. I can't go to prison. Please."

"Don't worry, fed time's not that bad," he mocked.

The first person that came to her mind was Jamir. Dazzle couldn't fathom going to prison and leaving her son behind with his less-than-responsible sperm donor. In just a blink of an eye, it felt as if her world started to crash before her eyes.

Detective Andrews pulled up at the light on Oakland Park Boulevard and made a left by the waterfall. Then he quickly stole a glance at his frightened passenger. "I mean, unless you ready to tell me who gave you this brick. I'm not interested in you small timers. I'll cut you a deal if you give me the name of your supplier."

Dazzle figured the best thing to do was to keep silent. To give Tori up was breaking the code, but losing her son was far worse than being labeled a snitch. All she needed was a phone call. Fresh or Tori were the only people who could get her out the mess she had just gotten into.

The car moved at a high rate of speed, flushing through traffic with the sirens blaring. Terrell pushed past the I-95 overpass and every other familiar road that led downtown to lock-up.

"Where are you taking me? The jail is in the opposite direction."

"Oh, did I say that's where I was taking you?" Terrell held his finger up. "I forgot to mention one thing to you."

"What's that?"

"Terry Andrews was my cousin. So, this, is personal for me."

"I told you don't know him."

Dazzle had finally broken and so did the dam that held her tears back. There was no doubt in her mind that she was about to die a slow and painful death. The same pain she subjected Terry to.

# Chapter 20

Tori unlocked the door to one of the units inside the duplexes that she had recently purchased. As usual, Honcho was attached to her hip like a colostomy bag. It was his duty to make sure she was protected at all times. Her heels click-clacked against the tile as she made her way around the semi-large apartment.

"What do you think?" She turned to face him.

"You already know I like it. All you need to do is upgrade the appliances in here and that's it."

"Yeah, I've been looking at some appliances online. I found this wholesaler in Davie and he said he'll give me a deal. We're going to go by there in a few days and see what he talking about. And to make sure the shit look good in person. It's easy to lie online."

"You already know these scammers everywhere." They walked to the back to check out the bedrooms again. It was a safety measure to ensure the original owner hadn't removed anything.

"Don't I know it? Lauderdale is the home of the scammers."

"When you trying to start renting?" Honcho peeked inside the closet.

"Sometime next week, I'm going to place an ad on *Craigslist* and see how that works. By the time they finish the application process, all of the units will be ready to move in."

"Not bad." Honcho stroked his jawline, as he walked behind Tori. The next stop was the bathroom.

Tori could feel his eyes burning a hole in her shirt. She stepped back out into the hallway. "What's on your mind?"

"What you mean?"

"Boy, as long as I've known you, I can tell when something going on in that head of yours."

Honcho was busted, with that Kool-Aid grin on his face. "I need to ask you a question."

"What's up?"

"We've been rocking for a long time, but now we're closer than ever before." Tori wasn't sure where the conversation was leading, but she continued to listen without interrupting. "I don't want to get into your business, but I feel like I need to. That's what I'm here for."

"Honcho, you're like my little brother. You can ask me anything and you know that."

"Are you being extorted for money?"

Tori was stunned by the assumption. "No. Why do you think that?"

"Who are you sending money to every month? I've noticed you deposit money into a bank account that doesn't belong to you. And I know it because I found a receipt."

Tori's eyes narrowed in on the empty space in the air between them. For the longest time she thought she was being discreet, but Honcho's line of questioning proved that theory to be wrong. Looking into his eyes, she knew it was out of love and not based on the intention of being nosy.

"I have personal affairs back in Georgia that I need taken care of while I'm away. My friend pays those things for me."

Honcho wasn't sure if he should believe her or not. It sounded like she was telling the truth. She had never lied to him before and there was no valid reason for her to be dishonest. Something just didn't sit right in his spirit, so he asked again for clarification.

"Are you sure nobody is extorting you? Don't lie to me."

Tori placed her hand on his shoulder. "It's nothing like that. I promise. If something like that was going on, I would tell you."

Honcho sighed with relief. "You had me worried for a second."

The sound of the door opening and closing put the duo on high alert. Honcho eased his 9mm handgun from his waistband and stepped in front of Tori, shielding her from any possible danger. The footsteps grew closer and closer. Unsure of what lie ahead, Tori pulled out her infamous Desert Eagle and took aim.

Honcho hit the corner and aimed it at the unknown man. "What the fuck you doing in here?"

"Who the fuck are you?" the man snapped back.

"Nigga, I'm asking the questions." Honcho held his aim steady.

Tori immediately recognized his voice and stepped into view to diffuse the situation. "Jude, what are you doing here?" She placed her hand on top of Honcho's hand, so he could put the gun away. "It's okay. I know him."

Jude's eyes were locked in on the man she was with. His face wasn't familiar and the two seemed awfully close. "I came to check on you to make sure you were okay." That lie rolled off his tongue quickly. The truth was, he had been watching her every move. "Who is this nigga?"

"Nigga, you see me standing here. Who the fuck is you?" Honcho matched his hostile tone.

"I'm her nigga, playboy," Jude boasted proudly.

"Okay. Okay. Both of you, stop it." Tori placed her hand on Honcho's chest. "This is my brother, Honcho."

Jude rubbed his tightening jawline. "Hmm, so this yo' brother-in-law huh? The one you always with. This shit funny."

Honcho was losing his patience by the second. He stepped closer to get his point across. "Nigga, you heard what the fuck—" Tori cut him off mid-sentence and blocked his path.

"Again, this is my brother."

"What you stopping him for? He ain't 'bout that," Jude smirked.

"Bruh, we can take this shit to the streets right now."

Tired of the back and forth, Tori stepped in front of Jude and pushed him towards the door. "Honcho, stay in here. I'll be right back."

"Oh, you making me leave?" Jude's back touched the door.

"Jude, listen to me. I'm not doing this right now. I have work to do and all this back and forth is unnecessary." Tori opened the door and the two of them walked outside.

Jude walked to the end of the sidewalk and stopped. When he turned to face Tori, he had a slight mug on his face. "Baby, why you always with this nigga?"

"Jude, how many times do you think I'm going to have this conversation with you?" Tori folded her arms and returned the same mug. Hers was just a little bit meaner. "All this jealous shit you got going on, I can't tolerate that."

"I know, baby, and I'm sorry." Jude placed both hands on her shoulder. "You being here with him just caught me off guard. I didn't know who it was and I just overacted."

"This the second time you've had to apologize. And something tells me this won't be the last." Tori moved his hands. "I've never been with a jealous man. As a matter of fact, Kilo was the only man I'd even been with."

"Just hear me out for a few minutes and I'll leave."

"Okay."

\*\*\*

Marcus was sitting at the park, getting his hustle on. The store was hot with police, so he had to set up elsewhere. After being out in the tethering heat for hours, he had managed to rack up six thousand dollars. With his back towards the main road, he separated his money and placed it in two different pockets.

"Today was a good day," he smirked. "All I need now is some pussy and head."

Marcus dialed a number on his phone and let it ring until the caller picked up. "Hello."

"Mya!"

"Who is this?" Mya rolled her eyes.

"This Marcus. Damn, you erased my number?"

"I got a new phone. What's up?"

"Let me come by and scoop you up." Marcus grabbed the crotch of his pants. "I'm 'bout to get a room and I want you to come with me."

"Nah. I can't."

"Damn, it's like that?"

"Me and my baby daddy back together."

"Word? That nigga out? No wonder why you been MIA on a nigga." Marcus was surprised. He was unaware that Tron had touched down. Mya and Marcus met on his multiple trips to McDonald's. The two had been kicking it for about a year. All of that changed when Tron hit the streets.

"Yeah."

"A'ight. Well, good luck with that."

"Bye." Mya hung up the phone fast.

"Well, let me call my back-up." Marcus dialed another number in his call log.

"Heyyy, Marcus," Tasha sang through the phone.

"What you doing?"

"Nothing. What's up?"

"I'm about to get a room. You gone let me scoop you up so I can dig in them panties?"

Tasha giggled. "You so nasty. What time you picking me up?"

"I'll be there in like thirty minutes."

"Okay. I'm about to get ready."

"Make sure that thang fresh too," he laughed.

"Boy, my shit always smell good. Don't play."

"I'm just fuckin' wit' you, chill out."

"Oh, I know."

"A'ight. I'll call you when I'm outside."

"Okay." Marcus was beaming when he hung up the phone. He was ready to slide by the liquor store and get a room. Head was overdue and he couldn't wait to go deep diving in Tasha.

"Scheduling a pussy appointment?" the voice behind him asked.

Marcus turned around and standing in front of him were some familiar faces. "Fuck y'all want?"

Zack stepped an inch closer, closing up the space in between them. "How much money you made tonight?"

"None of your fuckin' business." Immediately, Marcus cursed himself for leaving his gun in the car.

"That's where you wrong at." Zack took off and landed a quick punch to Marcus' nose, dazing him.

The rest of the crew jumped in and delivered vicious blows to Marcus' face and body. He was outnumbered, as he collapsed to the ground. Lying on the ground, he balled up and shielded his face. Zack and his boys stomped and kicked him repeatedly. The torturous beating lasted roughly around two minutes. They stopped abruptly and watched him squirm on the ground.

Zack leaned down and ran through his pockets, stealing his money. Marcus attempted to stop him but was unsuccessful. "Come on, man. Fuck you doing?"

"Nigga, what it look like? Robbing yo' punk ass."

"You don't wanna do that. You don't know who money you fuckin' wit," Marcus pleaded.

"Yeah, I do." He released a sinister laugh. "Yo' bitch ass work for Tori. Tell her the next time she decides to step on someone else's territory, think again. Take this as a warning, 'cause next time there will be bloodshed." Zack and his boys took off running and fled the scene.

Blood dripped from Marcus' lip. The soreness of his ribs made it hard for him to get up. Pushing the idea of the pain to the back of his mind, he struggled to get on his feet. Grateful they didn't take his phone, he dialed Tori's number to tell her what just occurred.

***

Tori was enraged when she ended the call with Marcus. Not only was he hit, but so were a few of her boys in the city. "I have to go. I'll talk to you later."

Jude was skeptical by the sudden swing on her mood. "Is everything okay?"

"No. But it will be."

"I can go with you," he insisted.

"I'll be okay. It's about business."

"Okay."

Tori rushed back into the apartment. Upon entering, she could see the baffled expression on Honcho's face just as he was ending the call he was on. "What's wrong? Is everything okay?" she asked.

"We have a problem."

"What's going on?"

"I just got off the phone with Fresh and he can't find Dazzle. She left the house early this morning to make a delivery and she never showed up."

Tori unlocked her cell. "I'm going to call her."

"He's been calling her and it's going straight to voicemail."

"Damn, it is," she sighed.

"You think she got locked up?"

"I hope not. I'm about to call and see."

"Do that in the truck. We need to get out of here and see what the fuck going on at the spots." Tori locked up the apartment, so they could leave.

Before calling the jail house, Tori reached out to her father-in-law. The phone rang a few times before he picked up, but there was silence on the opposite end. "Hello. Hello?"

"Yeah, baby. I'm here. What's up?"

"I need help."

"What's going on?" Eazy could hear the seriousness in her voice.

"We're on our way there now, so don't leave."

"I'll be here."

"Okay. See you soon."

# Chapter 21

Tori and Honcho walked into the living room, where Eazy and Fabian were sitting on the sofa having a drink. Eazy sat his glass down on the coffee table and took a deep breath. "What's going on? It sounded urgent."

Tori sat down and placed her purse beside her. "There's so much going on, I don't know where to start. First, two of my workers were robbed earlier by one of Diesel's workers. Now we can't find Dazzle."

Eazy turned his head slightly. "What do you mean you can't find her?"

"She had a delivery early this morning and never made it. Every time I call her phone, it goes straight to the voicemail and I don't know what to do." Tori's lips were moving a mile a minute.

"You think she was kidnapped? Or that she got locked up?" Eazy was thinking of possible options he could act on to help find her best friend.

"I don't know. This isn't like her. I did call downtown and she was never booked."

"I'm sure she'll turn up." Eazy assured his shaken daughter-in-law.

"I hope so." Tori sighed. "There's too much happening at one time and I cannot think straight."

"What are you gonna do about the hits on your team? You know you have to send a message. I'm here if you need my help." Eazy leaned forward. "What about Jarvis? Have you seen him?"

Tori shook her head. "No. I haven't seen him. From what I hear, he's been hiding."

"I'm gone kill his ass when I catch him." Eazy picked up his glass from the table.

"You should. He's the one that shot Kilo," she blurted out.

Eazy, Fabian and Honcho had surprised looks on their faces.

"What?" Honcho sat up in his seat.

"How do you know?" Eazy's blood began to boil.

"Sherrod told me." Tori could no longer keep the valuable information to herself. In reality, she wanted to be the one to kill him, but that was hard to do, since he went into hiding.

"That fuck nigga!" Honcho shouted.

"Sherrod?" Eazy frowned. "Where is he now?"

"Dead."

"What happened to him?" Eazy was curious.

Time was suddenly at a standstill and the room was silent. Tori's heart began race. It would be the first time she told anyone about the deed she had done, all in the name of love. Her eyes were locked in with his and her mouth opened slightly, as the words fell out slowly. "I killed him."

"What happened? Why didn't you tell me? The last thing I need is for your hands to get dirty. Or even worse, you end up in prison." Eazy wanted to kill everyone that had a hand in his son's death.

"No one saw me and I didn't say anything because it was spur of the moment." She looked away. "One night, I was driving alone and I saw him at a gas station. I followed him and confronted him about it. He admitted that Diesel wanted them to kidnap him. Sherrod tried to snatch him up, but Kilo shot him. After that, Jarvis shot him twice."

"Bruh, I think it's time for us to pay this nigga a visit," Eazy stated, while walking over to the nearby chest and pulling out two handguns.

Fabian couldn't agree more, but there was one slight problem that could possibly get in the way. "Jarvis has been in hiding since the day he told you about Diesel's snake ass. I've been looking for that young nigga high and low."

"Of course he's hiding. That fuck nigga know what he did. He handed me Diesel and Sherrod on a silver platter, just to keep his name out the mix."

Fabian wasn't sure how they were going to find him, but he was down for whatever. "So, what's the plan?"

"We gone bring that nigga out of hiding." Eazy tucked one of his guns into the waistband of his pants.

"Shiidd, let's do it then." Fabian stood to his feet.

"Keep trying to see if y'all can locate Dazzle, and Tori, I think it's best if you stay here for the night." Eazy refused to let Tori out of his sight. It was his job to protect his daughter since the day Kilo left her alone in the wicked world.

"Okay," she nodded her head.

Eazy and Fabian hopped into the car right at nightfall, on a desperate hunt to locate the sneaky weasel. The streets of Pompano were eerily dark and quiet. That was out of the ordinary for the busy city. Nonetheless, it didn't bother Eazy one bit. The way he was feeling, he would've smoked Jarvis in the middle of a crowd. With his eyes trained on every corner, and every dude they rode past, his mind was constantly on Kilo. There wasn't a day, an hour, a minute or a second that went by and he didn't think of him.

For the past few years, Eazy waited impatiently until he received all the answers he needed from the cold case. Street justice was the only way he could attempt to move on with his life. No matter the consequences, Eazy was getting revenge.

Fabian cruised up the block slowly. "Which house is it?"

"The yellow and white one coming up."

Fabian parked the car and checked their surroundings. A car was coming up the block, so they waited for it to pass. When the street was clear, they exited the vehicle. The lights were on, so that indicated someone was certainly home. Eazy tapped on the door and they stepped out of view.

"Who is it?" No one said a thing. "Who is it?" They kept quiet.

Eazy raised his gun when he heard the door open. That was when he stepped back into view, pointing the gun in the man's face. Fabian was right behind him. "Back up," Eazy demanded.

The man did as he was told and backed up with his hands in the air. "We ain't got no money, man. What y'all want?"

"Sit down," Eazy instructed. "Where's Jarvis?"

"Man, we haven't seen Jarvis. I don't know what type of shit he in, but we don't have anything to do with that."

"Walter, who you talking to?" The old lady walked into the living room. She was startled by the presence of the unknown men standing in her home, wielding guns. "What on earth is going on?"

Fabian pointed at the old lady. "Come sit next to him on the couch."

"Who else is here?" Eazy asked.

"My sister, but she sleep," Walter replied.

"Walter, who are these men?" his mother asked.

"I don't know, Ma. They looking for Jarvis." Walter looked Eazy squarely in the eyes. "Listen, we can't help you find Jarvis. We haven't seen or talked to him."

Eazy wasn't buying it. "Call his phone and put it on speaker."

"And what if he don't answer?"

"Leave him a message." Eazy kept his gun trained on the uncle while he dialed the number.

Walter tried his nephew twice, but each time, there was no answer. So, when the voicemail picked up, he started to talk. "Aye man, I don't know what you done got yourself into, but these niggas over here looking for you. They got guns and—"

*Boc*!

The single bullet Eazy lodged in his brain cut his message short. Jarvis' grandmother screamed when she saw her son come to his demise. Fabian silenced her quickly. *Boc*!

Then, both men headed down the hallway. The first room was empty, but the second room had a sleeping woman who was snoring hard. Eazy stepped into the room and put a bullet in her head. *Boc*!

After checking the house for any other witnesses, they went back into the living room. Eazy looked at Fabian. "Burn this motherfucker down!" And walked out the door.

\*\*\*

Fresh frantically made multiple calls to everyone he knew, including Dazzle's friends. No one had seen or heard from her. He was trying his best to keep it together, especially in front of Jamir. The last thing he wanted to do was upset his stepson. Two things for sure and one thing was certain, he wasn't going to rest until he brought her home.

"We not going home?" Jamir asked from the passenger seat.

"No. I'm about to drop you off to your grandmother's house and then I'm going to see your mom."

"Is she okay?"

"Yes. She's fine."

Jamir sat back in the seat and finished playing his game. Fresh pulled up in the driveway of Dazzle's mother's house in North Lauderdale. "Come on, man. It's time to see Grandma."

"Okay."

They walked up to the front door and were greeted by Ms. Shalonda with a smile. "Hey, Grandma baby."

"Hey, Grandma." Jamir reached up to hug her.

"Go inside the house and I'll be right in." Ms. Shalonda closed the door and stepped out onto the porch. "Have you heard anything?"

Fresh frowned. "No. Not yet. I'm about to head out and look for her now."

Ms. Shalonda was dressed in a moo-moo. "You know his no-good-ass daddy is out of prison."

"Yeah. She told me." Fresh thought back to the day Dazzle told him that Tron was out. For some odd reason, she appeared afraid.

"I don't trust his ass. And if he did something to my damn baby, I'm gone kill that bitch." The mean expression on her face told him she was serious.

"You ain't gone have to, 'cause I'm gone kill that nigga."

"Do you know where his mama live?" she asked.

"No."

"I'll give you her address. Check over there and see if you can find him. If you can't find my daughter tonight, I'm going straight to the police in the morning."

"I'm going to do my best and find her." Fresh opened his phone, prepared to type. "What's the address?"

Ms. Shalonda provided him with the address. Grabbing Fresh by the arm, her voice trembled with fear. "Son, please find my baby."

"I will, Ma. I promise." Fresh hugged her tight after seeing the frightening look on her face. "I won't rest until I do." And he meant just that.

Fresh ate up the highway until he made it to his destination. With his eyes on the swivel, he looked for the matching numbers on the house. Halfway up the street, he spotted the house. But there was no one outside. Therefore, he kept driving. "I got you now, fuck nigga."

At the light, he made a quick decision to grab some wraps from the corner store, so he busted a U-turn and went back. After making his purchase, he went back outside and got into his car. As he sat there and rolled up a blunt, loud talking broke his concentration. Fresh looked up and observed a young, black male going inside the store. He looked familiar. Fresh grabbed his gun and stepped out of the car. Standing by the trunk, he looked through the glass and realized it was Tron.

"Got yo' bitch ass now," he mumbled.

Fresh walked to the rear door at the passenger side and pulled the handle. To his surprise, it was open. Fresh climbed inside and closed the door. Leaning all the way to the back, he made sure he was out of view. From the car he could see Tron conversing with the clerk. They laughed for a while before he finally came out. Tron jumped into the car and fired up the engine. Before he was able to put the car in gear, Tron felt a cold piece of steel against his temple. He froze.

Fresh's finger rested on the trigger. "Where is Dazzle?"

"I don't know. I haven't seen her." Tron was so scared, he damn near shitted on himself.

"Quit lying. What you did to her?" Fresh barked.

"I swear to God, I didn't do nothing to her. That's my babymama, man, I wouldn't hurt her."

"You sure about that?"

"I promise. I'm not lying. I still love that girl," Tron admitted, in hopes that it would keep him alive.

Fresh ignored his comment about loving Dazzle. It was irrelevant and he knew where her heart was. "If I find out you had anything to do with her disappearance, I'm going to kill your mama, Mya and your son. And after I feel like you suffered enough, I'm killing you last. Do I make myself clear?"

"Yes. Yes. You won't have to do that. I swear." Tron just wanted him out the car expeditiously.

162

To let him know that he was serious, Fresh slammed the pistol against his head twice, as a warning. Blood trickled from the side of his head. Tron was knocked unconscious. His body slumped in the driver's seat. In his heart, he felt Tron didn't have anything to do with it, so he would let him live for now. If evidence proved otherwise, he was a dead man and so were the ones he loved. Fresh left the store in a hurry to continue the search for his woman.

***

Tori found it difficult to fall asleep, knowing that her best friend was still missing. After Eazy's concern about her safety, she decided to stay and sleep in her room. With nothing left to do, she sat in the room, reading another entry from her mother's diary.

*February 6, 2008*

*Here we go again with the bullshit. Another session. Another lesson of the bullshit. Every day I lay on this couch, I get more and more frustrated. If it wasn't my baby girl, Tori, I wouldn't be doing this shit at all. She is my world and I would do anything to be a better mother to her. Sometimes I feel like a failure, but the love Tori shows me, tells me otherwise. I remember when I found out I was pregnant with her. Diesel was so happy and so was I. We couldn't wait to be parents. He was the love of my life and I would've had a hundred babies if he wanted me to.*

*Anyway, Tori's birthday is less than a month away and I can't wait to celebrate her Sweet 16 with her. I'm in the middle of planning her the best birthday party she's ever had. My baby is so perfect and I owe her the world. Hopefully, I get to spend it with her. For days, I've been having these dreams of Diesel killing me with some bad dope, because that's only way he can get away with it. And something tells me that day is coming soon. I just pray it's after the party. I need to be present to see the happiness on her face.*

*God, if you can hear the prayers of a junkie like me, please show my daughter that I wasn't always this way. I was a good girl. I excelled in school. I graduated at the top of my class in high school and college. That was how I became a successful pharmacist. I just fell in love with the wrong man. He cheated on me and his mistress shot me in the stomach, killing my unborn son. That hoe is in prison now, but if I could get my hands on her, I would kill that bitch.*

*God, please protect my daughter, because she has been shielded from so much in life. There's so much she doesn't know about our past and it's scary. I'm sure she would be upset if she knew half of the shit that went down. From the beef between her father and Eazy, and the woman who's responsible for taking her baby brother. I've always wanted to come clean and let her know, but Diesel thought it was best to keep that part of our lives away from her. He could really be an asshole at times, but I could never muscle up the strength to leave him. I stayed because I wanted both of our kids to grow up in a two-parent household. The same way I did. So, for them I was willing to stick it out.*

Tori was distraught after she read that passage. Heavy tears were falling from her eyes. The mixed emotions she had were taking a toll on her. Seven years later and the pain was fresh, like Bianca died yesterday. "Mommy, I miss you so much. I love you. I've always loved you. Your addiction never changed my love for you and in my eyes, you were the best mother."

In the back of the diary was a picture of Bianca and Tori during happier times. Smiling at the priceless memory, she wiped her tears away. "If Diesel is responsible for your death, I swear, I will kill him for you." That wasn't a threat. It was a promise. Tori couldn't go through life knowing Diesel was responsible for taking away her number-one girl. It just didn't feel right.

Tori sat on the bed, still clutching the diary. There were so many questions she needed answers to. Just the thought of Diesel keeping secrets made it worse. He had already hit her with his secret family, so she knew the other secrets had to be far worse. Tori's mind was racing. Therefore, she couldn't read another page. Once she decided to call it a night, she placed the diary underneath her pillow and closed her eyes.

# Chapter 22

### The next day

"Ouu! Jarvis. Jarvis. My stomach," Lisa moaned out loud. Her hand cradled the bottom of her full belly. Jarvis didn't give her breakfast a chance to digest before he started digging up in her guts. The intense pressure of Jarvis nailing her from behind was painful for the expecting mother.

"Hush! The baby alright," he groaned in between each breath he took.

Jarvis was so caught up in the moment, to where it was impossible for him to slow down his strokes. There was so much stress in his life, and he needed to take it out on somebody. And at that moment, Lisa was his only option. Jarvis held onto her shoulders, as he dug deep with every stroke.

Lisa's arms grew weak. She desperately wanted to lay down, but that wasn't possible with their bundle of joy in the way. Fixated on pleasing her man, she sucked it up and leaned down as far as she could. Lisa's breasts hung freely. Her nipples grazed the mattress, sending pleasant tingles over her body.

Ignoring the sound of his phone, Jarvis smacked her ass. "Turn over. Ya ass look tired." Happy to change positions, Lisa quickly rolled onto her back. Pushing her legs open, he massaged her clit. Jarvis then slid his heavily coated piece back into her wet nookie.

Lisa's body succumbed to his touch and went into autopilot. Now able to enjoy the sex, Lisa could feel a pleasurable tingling sensation stimulating from her middle. Her legs trembled as she reached a heavy climax. Creamy fluids poured out her middle. Panting, she gripped the sheets. "Ahh! Mmm. Sss."

Jarvis continued to grind and slow stroke the kitty until he reached his peak. Squeezing her thighs, he pumped until she milked him for every drop. Lying down beside her, he took a deep breath. "Who the fuck keep calling me?" He snatched it up with an attitude. "Damn, a nigga can't nut in peace."

Unlocking his device, he glanced at the four missed calls and an urgent text from Moon. With no further delay, he hit him up. "Aye, I been trying to reach you."

"I'm at the house chillin'. What's going on?"

"You need to get up. I'm on my way over there. It's an emergency." Moon was flushing it on the highway.

"Talk to me, shit. What's good?"

"I hate to be the bearer of bad news," Moon sighed. "But your grandma house burned down sometime last night."

Those words drifted into his ears, but he hadn't processed what he was saying. Nor were those the words he was expecting to hear. Jarvis sat still in a state of shock.

"Bruh, did you hear what I said? Say something, fam."

"What happened?" Jarvis' voice was frail.

"I don't know. When I rode past there, they was putting out the fire. They had already brought out the bodies in body bags."

"My grandma dead?" Jarvis released the most horrific scream from the pit of his stomach. He rocked back and forth on the edge of the bed. "Nah. Not my grandma."

"I know, bruh. Try and stay calm. I'm about to pull up on you right now. I'm almost there." Moon knew it was hard on Jarvis. Therefore, he had to be at his side.

"Aight." Jarvis hung up the phone and dropped it on the floor. Covering his face with the palms of his hands, Jarvis closed his eyes and sobbed at his tragic loss.

The loss of his family members was something he never saw coming. In his eyes, laying low was something he felt would solve his problems. Ultimately, he was wrong. Lisa cautiously made her way over to comfort her man. Gently, she draped her arm across his back and rubbed it.

"I'm so sorry, baby. I'm going to help you get through this. I promise." Lisa's heart ached because his family showed nothing but love whenever she was around. They were even happy about the baby. Which was more than she could say about her own family.

Jarvis laid his head in the middle of Lisa's breasts, while she caressed his scalp and recited the 23rd Psalm. Through his cries, they could hear multiple knocks on the door. "I'll get it," Lisa said softly.

"Nah. Stay here. I got it." Jarvis stood up and left the room in a hurry, but not without grabbing his pistol from the dresser.

Moon walked through the front door and hugged Jarvis tight. "I love you, bro, and I'm here for you, woe. I'm riding with you until the end. Your family was my family."

"Thanks, fam. I needed to hear that." Jarvis took a step back and closed the door. "I'm about to grab my keys. I need to get over there."

Moon shook his head in disagreement. "Nah. You don't need to go over there right now. That place is swarming with cops. Trust me. Let that shit die down."

Lisa stepped foot into the living room and handed Jarvis his phone. "Jude just called you."

Jarvis grabbed the phone and hit his cousin back. "Wassup, cuz?"

"You heard about Grandma them?" Jude's voice was loud, coming through the speaker.

"Yeah. I did," he somberly stated.

Jude was heated and cut straight to the chase. "Did you have anything to do with that shit?"

"Fuck no! Why would you say some shit like that?" Jarvis loved his family and wouldn't put them in harm's way intentionally.

"'Cause nigga, you messy as fuck in these streets. And for someone to kill our grandma, auntie and uncle execution-style, has the streets written all over it. So, tell me what the fuck you got yourself into?"

Jarvis jumped to his feet. "What? I thought they died in a house fire. What the fuck you talkin' about?"

"They were killed before the fire. So, again, who the fuck you beefing with?" Jude placed the clip into his firearm.

"I ain't beefing with nobody." Jarvis knew he did some shady, snake-ass shit in the streets, but he wasn't about to admit that shit to Jude. He also had an idea of who was behind the executions.

"I ain't beefing with nobody."

Jude shook his head and sat his gun beside him on the sofa. "For some reason I don't believe that shit."

"I'm not beefing with nobody. I swear," he lied.

"A'ight. If I find out they got killed behind some shit you started, you gone meet the same fate, lil cuz, and I promise you that." Jude knew Jarvis had a bad rep in the streets. Therefore, he knew his word couldn't be trusted.

"Cuz, listen to me. I had nothing to do with this shit. I swear to you I didn't."

"You better hope not. Or I'm gone forget we family. I swear." Jude hung up the phone abruptly.

Jarvis stared at the screen in fear. In his heart, he knew who was behind the hit. He just prayed it didn't get back to Jude. If the truth was to ever surface, Jarvis knew it was kill or be killed. However, his gut told him the whole ordeal wouldn't end well.

Moon stared into the eyes of his closest friend and could feel the pain in his heart. "You good, fam? What that nigga hollerin' about?"

"He gone kill me if I had something to do with these murders."

Moon sat up at attention. "Tell me this don't have nothing to do with you?"

Jarvis shook his head. Then slowly, he raised his head to meet Moon eye-to-eye, with tears falling. "I wish I could."

"Damn, fam, what we gone do?" Moon couldn't let Jarvis go down on his own. They were more than friends. They were brothers. And he loved him as if his own mother birthed him.

"We gotta get rid of Diesel. He's behind this and I know it."

"How you figure?" Moon was trying to connect the dots.

"I told Eazy that Diesel was behind Kilo's death. That's why my ear fucked up now."

"You know you not about to get close to Diesel. That ain't happening."

"I know that." Jarvis stared at Moon with a menacing stare on his face. "That's why we have to snatch his daughter up, so he can come to me."

"I'm 'bout that. What we gone do?"

Jarvis rubbed his hands together. "I have a plan."

168

***

Dazzle was slumped in a daze, seated in a chair, until she felt like she was drowning. In a panic, she shook her head in an effort to save her own life from the water that threatened to take her under. When she opened her eyes, Terrell was standing in front of her with an evil smirk plastered on his face.

"Nice of you to join me, sunshine," he smiled. "I thought I lost you for a minute."

Dazzle struggled to move, but soon realized she was bound by her arms and legs by one of those black leather sex chairs she saw online, when trying to find items to spruce up her and Fresh's sex life. "Please," she cried. "You don't have to do this."

"I know I don't, but I want to." Terrell pulled a pocketknife from his pocket and flicked the blade into the upward position. "I'm the law around here and that means I can do what the fuck I wanna do." He then ran the blade across her thigh. "I mean, unless you want to tell me who you working for."

"Nobody. I'm a single mother and I have to make a way for me and my son," she pleaded with lies.

"Bullshit!" he stated coldly. "Now let's try this again."

"I'm telling you the truth," she repeated.

Terrell continued to slide the blade until he reached her belly button. Dazzle began to tremble with fear, as he cut open her shirt. Pressing the knife into her skin, he slid the cold blade across her perky breasts. The sight of blood made her weak, as it broke her skin. "Please don't kill me," she begged.

"I'm not going to kill you just yet. I'm not letting you off that easy." Terrell punched her in the face. "Bitch, you gone suffer for the shit you and your friend did to my cousin."

Terrell bent down to the floor and picked up a bottle of alcohol. Twisting off the cap, he poured the liquid over her open wound. Dazzle screamed out in agony from the burning sensation. To take her mind off the pain, she closed her eyes and thought about Jamir.

# Chapter 23

Tori was awakened to a strong, heavy knock on the door. She blinked several times before sitting upright. "Come in," she yawned.

The door creaked open slowly. Honcho peeped in before walking all the way through the door. "I didn't wake you up, did it?"

"It was time for me to get up anyway. What's up?" she yawned again.

Honcho walked over to the bed and sat down. "What time you wanna head out to handle this business?"

"I'm about to get up and shower now. But I want to go out and check a few spots to see if anyone heard from Dazzle. We have to find her."

"We will," he sighed, feeling her pain. "I just got off the phone with Fresh and he's headed back out to look for her."

"Where is Jamir?"

"He's with Dazzle's mom," he replied.

"I'm willing to bet Tron had something to do with this. That ungrateful, no-good bitch." Tori picked up her phone to see if she had any missed calls. There were several, but none of them were from Dazzle. They were all from Jude. Just as she sat the phone down, it rang. Quickly, she sent him to voicemail.

Honcho tried to see whose call she was dodging. "That's your boyfriend calling?"

"Yeah."

Honcho frowned in disgust. "I don't like that dude. And I'm not saying that because I don't want you to move on. I'm saying it because he's too jealous and possessive. That's a recipe for disaster."

"He's not that bad," Tori attempted to defend him. "I mean, he's a good dude. Not to mention, he treats me well. He's just a little on the jealous side because of past relationships."

Honcho chuckled. "So, the nigga a bitch."

"No." She slapped him playfully on the arm. "He's definitely not that."

"I beg to differ, but okay." Honcho rose to his feet and headed towards the door. "I'll be downstairs waiting on you."

Tori waited until he closed the door before she crawled out of the king-sized bed, dressed in shorts and a tank top. Walking into the bathroom, she jumped into the shower. Hot and steamy was on the menu. Once her skin began to wrinkle, Tori decided it was time to get out. After wrapping up in a towel, she walked back into the bedroom and sat at the edge of the bed.

Tori used the next thirty minutes to lotion her body and get dressed. Once she was finished, she decided to call Jude back. Just as she picked up her phone, it started ringing. Sabrina's name popped up on the screen.

"Hey, boo. Is everything okay?"

"Umm. Is this Tori?" an unknown male asked.

"Yes. Who is this?"

"This James. I'm Sabrina's brother."

"Oh, hey." Tori was a tad bit confused as to why he would be calling her. "Where's Sabrina?"

"That's why I'm calling." He took a deep breath before revealing the reason for his call. "There's been an accident."

Tori's heart skipped a beat, as she panicked, thinking about the worst-case scenario. "An accident?"

James' voice trembled, as he tried to explain. "She was in a three-car collision on I-75."

"Is. Is she going to be okay? Was she alone?" Tori's thoughts were all over the place.

"Honestly, it's not looking good. She's in critical condition. I was watching the kids while she was gone." James wiped the tears from his eyes. "I know y'all had an arrangement, but I can't do this. I need you to—"

"I know," she closed her eyes to stop the tears. "I'm about to search for some flights and I'll be there."

"I'm sorry," he said sincerely.

"No. It's okay. This is long overdue." Tori opened her eyes and wiped her face with her hand. "I'll be there tonight."

"Thank you."

"No. Thank you for calling me."

"You're welcome."

Tori immediately left her room on the hunt for Eazy downstairs. Eventually, she found him in his bedroom, on his knees, reading the Bible. She stood there and listened.

"Then I saw a new heaven and a new earth, for the first heaven and the first earth had passed away, and the sea was no more. And I saw the holy city, New Jerusalem, coming down out of heaven from God, prepared as a bride adorned for her husband. And I heard a loud voice from the throne saying, Behold, the dwelling place of God is with man. He will dwell with them, and they will be his people, and God himself will be with them as their God. He will wipe away every tear from their eyes, and death shall be no more, neither shall there be mourning, nor crying, nor pain anymore, for the former things have passed away." Eazy stood up and stretched.

"Good morning. I hope I'm not interrupting," she sniffled.

"Not at all. Come in." Eazy pointed at the corner of the bed. Easily he sensed that something was wrong. "Are you okay?"

"No." She shook her head.

"Talk to me." Eazy gave her his full attention.

"I need to fly to Atlanta tonight." Tori was doing her best to contain her emotions. "My friend was in a car crash and she might not make it."

Eazy moved in close and hugged her tight. "I'm so sorry to hear that. What do you need from me?"

"Can you go with me? I don't want to go alone."

"Sure." Eazy promised to be there for her and that was exactly what he was going to do. "Find us a flight out and I'll pay for it."

Tori nodded her head. "Okay." When Eazy released her from his grip, she looked up at him with the saddest eyes. "Eazy."

"Yes."

"I have something I need to tell you first." Tori closed her eyes and prepared to drop a bombshell on him.

\*\*\*

Fresh had been on a hunt since Dazzle went missing. Every time he called her phone, it continued to go to the voicemail. If he didn't find her within the next few hours, Ms. Shalonda was going to report her missing. The last thing he wanted was to involve the police. Fresh was running on no sleep, and liquor from the night before. It was hard to sleep without Dazzle and not knowing if she was dead or alive.

Determined to end his search, he backtracked on the way she would normally travel. "Come on, baby. Tell me where you at. We need you."

Fresh cruised down 56th Avenue, doing the speed limit of thirty-five miles per hour. A tow truck was in the middle of the road blocking traffic. Tapping on the brake, he slowed down until he came to a complete stop. "Come on, man. Get this shit out the way."

After waiting for what seemed like forever, the tow truck finally moved. Fresh looked in the direction of the truck and that was when he was taken aback. The sight of Dazzle's car caught his attention. Slamming down on the gas, Fresh whipped his way into the parking lot and threw his car in park.

The driver froze when he saw Fresh speed walking in his direction, but he didn't say a word. "This my wife car. Where are you taking it?" Fresh looked around, hoping that Dazzle would appear. "And where is she?"

"Sorry buddy, I don't have that information. All I know is we received a call to pick up an abandoned car." The driver reached inside his shirt pocket and pulled out a business card. "This is where you can pick it up. If you have any questions, I would suggest talking to the hotel manager. He's the one who called."

"Thanks, man." Fresh jogged towards the hotel's entrance and approached the front desk.

"Good morning, sir, how can help you?" the front desk clerk asked.

"The car that's being towed," he pointed towards the window. "It belongs to my wife. Where is she?" Fresh halfway hoped she rented a room, so she could be alone. But deep down inside, he knew that wasn't the case.

"I'm sorry, sir, but I don't know." The young woman picked up the receiver. "Give me one moment and I'll call my manager."

"Okay."

Fresh waited impatiently until he was approached by the young manager. "Hello. How can I help you?" the manager asked.

Fresh studied his name tag before responding. "Charles, my wife's car is currently being towed, and I need to know why and her location."

Charles contemplated on if he should be honest, but there was no proof the man in front of him was telling the truth. Nor was there any indication that he was lying. "That car being towed because the owner does not have a room here. This is a no-trespassing zone."

"Charles, I think you bullshittin' me." Fresh moved in closer, but Charles took a step back. "And if you don't tell me what you know," Fresh looked around with an evil grin. "I would hate to see this building in flames and all over the news."

Charles was intimidated by the muscular, scary-looking man standing before him. "Yeah. Yeah," he stroked his beard. "As a matter of fact, I remember seeing a woman here yesterday. She was outside talking to a man. Then a few minutes later, he escorted her to his car and put her in the backseat."

"Are you saying she was arrested?" Fresh was skeptical about what he was hearing.

"I want to say yes, but there's no way to be sure. He wasn't in a patrol car. I mean, unless he was an undercover cop." Charles was almost certain the unknown man was indeed a cop, based on how he was dressed.

Fresh stood in place and scanned the lobby once more. "Do you have outside cameras?"

Charles folded his arms across his chest. "I'm sorry, but that footage is not available to the public. Only a detective can obtain that footage. So, I would suggest you visit the local police department to view it."

"In that case, let me show you my badge." Fresh reached inside his pocket, pulled out a stack of bills and waved it in his face. "My bad, I thought you took my question for permission."

"Um. Um." Charles didn't know what to say. He needed his job in order to provide for his family and really didn't want to take that risk.

Fresh firmly placed his hand on the manager's shoulder. "Listen to me, my wife is missing and I need to find her."

Charles felt like he was being truthful, so he quickly opened his mouth. "Okay," he agreed. "Just follow me into my office."

Fresh followed him down the hall and into a side office. Charles sat down at his desk, while Fresh stood over his shoulder. The room had an eerie silence as he waited on what the video would reveal. Clear as day, Fresh watched Dazzle enter the parking lot with a car close behind her. The lights on the front dash caught his attention. There was no doubt in his mind that the slender male who stepped from the black Charger was an undercover cop. His heart sank to the pit of his stomach as he continued to watch the events unfold.

# Chapter 24

"Babe, come on. Get in with us," Jenna laughed, while splashing water in her son's face.

Diesel stood underneath the gazebo, flipping the meat on the grill. He decided to take the day off and spend some quality time with his family. It would've been a joy to have Tori in attendance, but he knew that day would probably never happen. Hell would freeze over before Tori spent a day with them.

"I'm coming, give me a few minutes. I know you don't want no Cajun meat," he joked.

"Oh, I want your Cajun meat." Jenna licked her lips, while staring in her man's direction.

"I bet you do." Diesel grabbed his Heineken and started to walk through the grass towards the pool. Suddenly, he felt something hit his foot. Diesel jumped back when he spotted a black snake. "Oh shit!" he shouted.

"What's wrong?" Jenna asked.

"It's a fuckin' snake." Diesel ran back to the gazebo and grabbed a machete. By the time he returned to the spot, it was gone.

"Kill it," she screamed.

Determined to kill the creature, he crept slowly through the yard with his weapon clutched in his hand. A sound near the bushes by the wooden fence grabbed his attention. Diesel spotted the shiny creature and swung his blade, slicing it in half. Bending down, he picked it up and held both pieces in the air.

"This what I do to my enemies," he huffed. "I kill them bitches."

Jenna watched in disgust. "Eww. Put that thing in the garbage."

Diesel made his way towards the pool and dangled the snake over the water. "You wanna touch it?"

"Hell, no." She inched backwards in the water. He pretended like he was about to throw it in. Jenna screamed, "Diesel, stop playing so much."

"Hush. You know I'm not about to throw that in there, big-ass cry baby." Diesel discarded the snake into the trash can and washed his hands. Finally, he was able to join them in the pool for some fun in the sun.

*** 

Tori and Eazy left the airport in the rental car they had just picked up. It was a quarter after seven, so she called James to let him know that she was in town.

"Hello," he answered.

"Hey. I'm here. Where are you?" Tori asked.

"I'm at Sabrina's house. Visiting hours are over, so you can come here," James replied.

"I'm on my way."

"Okay. See you soon."

Tori hung up the phone and glanced over at Eazy. He was silent and staring out the window. "I can understand if you're upset with me. I couldn't be mad at you if I wanted to, because I brought this on myself. All I want you to understand is that I did all of this because I didn't have a choice. Just look at my life and the way I live."

Eazy reached over and grabbed Tori's hand. "I'm not upset with you. I understand your reasoning, but you should've known I would've been by your side and did all I needed to do to help you. You didn't have to lie to me."

Tori fought back the tears. "I know, but I had my reasoning. It was hard for me too. This wasn't something I wanted to do, but I had to protect what belongs to me. You see all the damage Diesel has caused."

"I do." Eazy nodded.

"Please forgive me."

"I do," he promised. "Just promise that you will never, ever lie to me again. No matter what it is."

"I promise." She meant exactly what she said.

Forty minutes later, they were pulling up to Sabrina's home. The same house Honcho dropped her off at during their business trip. She glanced over to the passenger seat and looked into Eazy's eyes. "Are you ready?"

"I'm more than ready." Eazy unbuckled his seatbelt and stepped from the rental car. Tori did the same.

Once at the door, Tori knocked and waited on an answer. Seconds later, James opened the door and she gave him a big hug. "Thank you so much for calling me."

"You're welcome."

Turning towards Eazy, she introduced the two men. "James, this is my father-in-law, Eazy."

"Hey, man, nice to meet you." James extended his hand.

"It's nice to meet you too." Eazy shook his hand before walking into the door.

"Where is he?" Tori asked.

"Upstairs," James informed her.

"Thanks." Tori looked back at Eazy and stated, "Follow me."

Tori and Eazy walked up the staircase slowly, one by one until they reached the top, and down the hall. Tori took a deep breath before opening the bedroom door. Her heart melted when she saw his warm smile and bright eyes. Instantly, he jumped up from the bed where he was watching television.

"Mommy, Mommy."

Tori dropped to her knees and hugged her baby boy tight. "I missed you so much, baby."

"I missed you too." Capone kissed her lips.

Tori looked into his big, brown eyes that reminded her of his father. "I would like you to meet someone. This is your grandfather, Eazy. He's your father's dad." Tori nudged him in Eazy's direction. "Say hi."

Capone looked up at Eazy and smiled. "Hi."

"Eazy, this is your grandson, Capone Kilo Kingsley."

Eazy started to shed tears as he laid eyes on his one and only grandson for the first time. "Damn, he looks just like Kilo."

"He does," Tori smiled.

Eazy leaned forward and picked up Capone. "This is bittersweet. I love you so much and we just met." Eazy hugged him tight and Capone returned the affection by embracing him.

"I wish your father could've met you." Eazy cried the same tears the way he did when Kilo died. Seeing Capone was like having Kilo back in the flesh. Extending his arm, he reached for his daughter-in-law.

Tori stepped in closer and laid her head on his chest. "I wish he was here too." A lone tear escaped her eye as he broke all over again.

\*\*\*

After Terrell ended his torture tactics on Dazzle, he went outside to retrieve her cellphone. Hitting the side button, he attempted to power on the phone, but it didn't come on. Inside the house, he rambled through a drawer until he found a charger. While the phone was juicing, he decided to make a call.

Marsha picked up the phone on the fourth ring. "Hello."

"You busy?"

"No. What's up?"

"I need you to come by the secret spot." Terrell spoke in a low voice, as if someone else was in the room.

"Hmm," Marsha grinned. "Is this a dick appointment?"

"Maybe," he chuckled. "You'll see when you get here."

"Okay. Give me like twenty minutes to get fresh for you and I'll be there."

"Alright."

Terrell ended the call and went back to Dazzle's phone. He was then able to power it on with no problem. To his surprise, there was no lock screen activated. Therefore, he was able to roam freely through the content. One name in particular sparked his interest, Tori.

"Tori," he mumbled. That was when he remembered doing a favor for his niece Whitney's friend, whose name was Tori.

Terrell then scrolled through the gallery. Immediately, he spotted Tori in one of the photos. It was definitely her. Quickly, he called in a favor. Once the call was over, he went back to where he held his victim. Dazzle was staring at the ceiling, praying for a miracle when her captor walked in whistling.

"Are you ready to talk now?" He stood beside her eyeing the fresh bruises on her body.

Dazzle was over the torture. "What do you want from me?" she panted.

"Tell me who you work for." Terrell raised his hand and she jumped. "Relax. I won't hit you again, unless you tell me what you want. And this time it will be worse and I will put your son in foster care."

Dazzle began to think hard about dropping Tori's name.

"Before you think about lying again, take a look at this." Terrell showed her a picture of Jamir. "If you want to see your son again, you'll start talking. Now, who do you work for?"

Wells of water began to form in Dazzle's eyes. Jamir was her life and she didn't trust anyone to love her son the way she did. All out of options she broke her silence. "Tori," she said just above a whisper.

"Tori who?"

"Tori Price."

"Is she related to Torin Price?" Terrell was no stranger to that name. In fact, Torin's name came across his desk on more than one occasion.

"That's her father." Dazzle felt like a snitch, but she had to save herself and her son. "Will you please let me go? I told you what you wanted."

"Not just yet." A plan so devious and genius crossed his mind. He knew he had to play his cards right of he wanted to come out on top. The petty hustler's money he took from Franklin Park wasn't merely enough. But now, he'd landed a bigger fish and he wanted more.

# Chapter 25

Tori and Eazy walked up the stairs of his home and stopped in front of Honcho's room door. Eazy looked back at Tori and Capone. "You ready?"

"Yes." She nodded her head.

Eazy knocked on the door and waited for his son to respond. Once he heard his voice, he opened the door. Honcho and Lala were lounging on the bed watching a movie when he walked in. "Turn off the TV, we need to talk."

Honcho grabbed the remote and powered it off. "What's up, Pops?"

"We're going to get to that, but I need you to have an open mind and not get upset," Eazy replied.

"Who is we?" Honcho was confused and so was Lala.

Eazy looked towards the door. "Come in, Tori." Tori walked in holding Capone's hand.

Honcho took one look at the child that was a spitting image of his brother. From his brownish complexion, down to his eyes, there was no doubt about their relation. "What's going on?"

Lala sat up in the bed. "Oh my God, he looks just like Kilo."

Tori stood beside the bed and looked her closest family members in the eyes. "This is Capone Kilo Kinglsey, me and Kilo's son." The puzzled look on their faces told her she needed to explain and explain fast.

"Before y'all say anything else, let me tell you what happened." Tori sat down on the bed and sat Capone in her lap. Taking a deep breath, she went back to what happened four years ago.

"Right before Kilo and I got married, I found out I was pregnant. I wanted to surprise him with the results of my pregnancy test, but I didn't get the chance to do that." The memory of Kilo's final moments started to weigh in on her and the tears started to fall. "He called me and I heard the gunshots. When I got there and I held him in his arms, I begged him not to leave me, to leave us."

Tori held Capone tight and kissed the top of his head. "That was when he told me he knew I was pregnant and if it was a boy, name him Capone." Tori became emotional and stopped talking.

Lala began to tear up as well and stood beside Tori, as she rubbed her back. "It's okay, Tori. Take your time."

Tori wiped her eyes and took a deep breath. "When I went off to college, my professor detected that I was pregnant and gave me some advice. I drove to the abortion clinic and once I was inside, I couldn't go through with it. I couldn't abort my child. I loved Kilo too much to do that. He was my world. Still is."

Tori wiped her wet eyes once more. "Just the thought of bringing his child into the world was worth the struggle. I needed to have a part of him on earth with me."

Honcho wiped his tears way as well. "I'm happy you kept my nephew, but I have so many questions."

Tori looked Honcho in the eyes. "I know you do, and I'll get to that. After I changed my mind, I went back to see my professor, Sabrina, and explained my situation to her. I told her I needed to finish college, but I needed help. She agreed to raise Capone and be his godmother, so I could finish school."

Lala had a question of her own. "Why didn't you bring him back with you after graduation?"

"I wanted to buy a house first and get myself situated before I did that," Tori replied.

"He could've came here," Honcho added.

"I know, but I didn't know how to tell all of you. Sabrina's brother called me and told me that she was in a car crash that left her paralyzed, so I had to go and get him. Eazy went with me." Tori saw Sabrina like a second mother and her heart was aching about the incident.

"When you asked me about who I was sending money to every month, this is who I was sending it to," she admitted.

"Damn," Honcho sighed.

"I'm sorry. I know this is a lot to take in, but I didn't know what to do. This was so hard for me, so please don't be upset."

"I'm not upset, sis. I just wish you would've said something sooner," Honcho stated with emotion.

"I'm not mad either. I'm happy." Lala placed a kiss on Tori's cheek. "I love you."

"I love you too," Tori replied.

Capone looked up and rubbed Tori's face. "Don't cry, Mommy." He then looked around at the unfamiliar faces. "Mommy, who are these people?"

Tori couldn't help but to laugh through her tears. "This is Lala, your other godmother and this is your uncle Honcho, your father's brother." Honcho reached for Capone and surprisingly, he went to him.

Squeezing him tight, Honcho kissed his nephew. "My brother would've been a good father. You look so much like him."

Tori's heart was filled with so many emotions, but there was still one more person she needed to talk to. Rising to her feet, she looked at Eazy. "I need to come clean to one more person and then this will all be over." Eazy nodded his head.

Tori looked at Lala. "I'm going to need your help."

Lala looked into Tori's bright, red eyes with a smile on her face and replied, "Anything." Tori left the room to make a call.

\*\*\*

Tori paced the living room of the old house she and Kilo once shared. Old memories of her and her husband flooded her mind. So many great things happened at that address, including the conception of Capone. On the tragic side, it was where the tragedy that claimed Kilo's life took place.

"Kilo, baby, the closing for this house is taking place as we speak. I'll never let go of the memories we created here. Especially, our handsome ass son. I promise to be the best mother I can be."

The sound of a car pulling up interrupted all of her thoughts. Tori looked out the window and saw he was on time, as expected. Her heart began to race. The palms of her hands became sweaty. Tori wiped her hands along the side of her jeans as she struggled to keep her composure. "You can do this. You can do this," she repeated over and over again, as she opened the door and stood in the frame.

Diesel walked up to the door and gave Tori the biggest hug. It had been weeks since he'd last seen his daughter. "I'm so glad you called me."

"Come in." Tori stepped back and let him in. She closed the door and did an about-face. "Have a seat."

Diesel sat down and crossed his legs. "It's so good to see you baby. What was so urgent that you needed me to come over? You know I'm here for you, no matter what it is."

Tori sat down in the single fold-out chair that sat in the middle of the floor. "You know I wish I could believe that, but I don't."

Diesel was puzzled about her response. "What do you mean? I've been by your side since the day your mother had you."

Tori shook her head. "Have you really?"

"Yes. I have. The only thing I'm guilty of is being an overbearing father and that's only because I love you. I've loved you since the day I knew your mother was expecting you."

Hate and anger wrapped around Tori's heart like a valve with intense pressure. "Somehow, I don't believe you."

"You should."

"At this moment, I'm going to forget about the lies that are spewing from your mouth like a venomous snake. I'm older and I know better. I'm going to get to the reason I brought you here."

"And what's that?" Diesel ignored her evil words in order to get down to the nitty gritty.

"Just like you, I've been keeping a four-year secret from you and it's time to come clean. Unlike you, I need to clear my conscience."

"And what would that be?" Diesel was skeptical about what his baby girl had to tell him.

"Lala, come out!" Tori screamed. Lala walked out with Capone in her arms.

Lala placed him down beside Tori. "Here you go."

Before he could say anything, Tori began to talk. "I would like for you to meet your grandson."

Diesel's eyes widened in surprise. "My who?"

"Your grandson." Tori pulled her son close to her. "When I went off to college, I was pregnant. My professor raised him so I could finish school. This is me and Kilo's son."

"Wait, what?" Diesel scratched his head. "My grandson."

"Yes. I had a baby while I was away," Tori snapped.

"Why didn't you tell me?"

"For what? So, you could talk me out of it?" Tori was angry all over again.

Diesel contemplated about his response. The accusations she spat were true, but he wouldn't admit to that. His guilt wouldn't allow it. "No. I would've wanted to be there for you." Diesel sat upright, "What's his name?"

The toddler spoke up on his own. "My name is Capone."

"Come here." Diesel extended his arms.

Capone was as friendly as they came. "Can I, Mommy?"

"Yes," she replied.

Capone walked over and stood in front of his grandfather with a curious eye. "What's your name?"

"Grandpa Diesel."

"Hi, Papa Diesel," Capone smiled. He was the happiest kid anyone could ever meet. Diesel hugged him tight.

Tori gave them all of two minutes together, before she interrupted their session. "Lala, take him in the back."

"Okay," Lala replied. "Come on, Capone. Let's go."

When they left the room, Tori laid it out on the line. Her eyes roamed the room before she began to speak. "Do you know Kilo bought this house for me?"

"No. I didn't know that," Diesel answered quickly.

"I know you don't." Tori had the meanest mug plastered on her grill. "When Kilo was killed, that was the worst day of my life. I wanted to die right along with him, because I knew there would never be another man on earth that would love me the way he did. But you took that away from me."

Diesel appeared shocked, but he knew exactly what she was talking about. "What are you talking about? I didn't take him away from you."

Tori grunted and rocked in her seat. "Stop lying to me," she screamed.

"I'm not," he rebutted quickly.

"You are." Tori jumped from her seat and pulled out the signature gold Desert Eagle that once belonged to Kilo. "You killed the love of my life."

Diesel held up both hands. "No, I didn't. Put the gun away. Please."

"No. You broke my heart and now I'm going to bust yours." Tori's finger rested comfortably on the trigger.

"Tori, please. I'm your father, don't do this," he pleaded.

"Fuck that." Tori put a round in the chamber. "Lala, come back out here."

Lala closed the door where Capone was watching cartoons and entered the bedroom. "You ready?"

"Yes." Tori stepped to the side with her gun still aimed. "Sit in this chair. And don't try anything or you will die here today."

Diesel sat down in his appointed seat without a fight. Tori kept her gun aimed at him, while Lala tied him up. In his mind, he felt like Tori wouldn't pull the trigger, but his mind said otherwise. He hoped his love for her outweighed the hate she had for him. When Lala was done, she looked at Tori.

"You want us to leave now?" she asked.

"Yes," Tori replied. Lala grabbed Capone and they left out the back door.

Tori sat down on the sofa. She was distraught and upset about everything she learned about her father. Her behavior was hysterical and unattainable. However, she tried to keep it together for the sake of the truth.

"I'm going to ask you some questions and I need you to be honest with me." Tori was ready for him to lie at any moment. "I'm going to ask you a series of questions and you better be honest."

"Okay." Diesel nodded.

"Did you kill Kilo?" Tori's heart raced with anticipation.

"No."

Tori rubbed her temple. "Why are you lying?"

"I'm not."

"That's a lie," snapped. "I spoke with Sherrod, right before I killed him, and he told me he had an order from you to kidnap and kill Kilo."

Diesel knew his words wouldn't hold water when it came to his daughter, but he knew he had to be honest. "Tori, I swear, I had nothing to do with his death. On everything I love, I only told them to kidnap him and bring him to me. I knew he wouldn't come willingly. I had to make him come to me and that was the only way. Tori, I swear, all I wanted to do was talk to him about making you go to college. By the time we spoke, it was too late to call it off. They were already there. I couldn't stop it."

Tori sat in silence as she cried. No matter what Diesel said, it was his fault Kilo was dead. "You killed my husband. The day you had your fake ass goons come here, we had just gotten married at the courthouse. You ruined my life," she screamed.

"I'm sorry, baby. That wasn't my intention." Diesel stated honestly.

"No. You keep that sad ass apology. You purposely ruined my life and now I'm going to ruin yours and your bastard child." Tori aimed her gun at Diesel and pulled the trigger. *Boca!*

\*\*\*

"Did you hear that shit?" Jarvis asked, while looking over in the passenger seat at Moon.

"That sounded like a gunshot," Moon replied, as he stared at the front door.

"Yeah, but now my question is, who pulled the trigger?" Jarvis was skeptical about he'd just heard.

"Shit, I'm out here with you." Moon stroked the barrel of his gun. "We know Tori in there, but I know Diesel would never kill his daughter."

"Just like she won't kill her daddy." Jarvis rubbed his head. "It's somebody else in that house. We just don't know who it is."

"I agree. Them muthafuckas just killed somebody." Moon sat his gat on his lap.

"Well, we sitting right here until she come out. I'm still snatching that bitch up just as soon as she's alone." Jarvis pulled out a cigarette and lit it. As they lie in wait, Jarvis peeped a familiar truck pull up. On edge, he watched closely as a familiar face stepped out of the vehicle. "What the fuck going on?" Jarvis mumbled.

To Be Continued
Dope Girl Magic 3
Coming Soon!

# Submission Guideline

Submit the first three chapters of your completed manuscript to ldpsubmissions@gmail.com, subject line: Your book's title. The manuscript must be in a .doc file and sent as an attachment. Document should be in Times New Roman, double spaced and in size 12 font. Also, provide your synopsis and full contact information. If sending multiple submissions, they must each be in a separate email.

Have a story but no way to send it electronically? You can still submit to LDP/Ca$h Presents. Send in the first three chapters, written or typed, of your completed manuscript to:

**LDP: Submissions Dept**
**Po Box 944**
**Stockbridge, Ga 30281**

*DO NOT send original manuscript. Must be a duplicate.*

Provide your synopsis and a cover letter containing your full contact information.

Thanks for considering LDP and Ca$h Presents.

## Coming Soon from Lock Down Publications/Ca$h Presents

BOW DOWN TO MY GANGSTA

By **Ca$h**

TORN BETWEEN TWO

By **Coffee**

THE STREETS STAINED MY SOUL **II**

By **Marcellus Allen**

BLOOD OF A BOSS **VI**

SHADOWS OF THE GAME II

By **Askari**

LOYAL TO THE GAME **IV**

By **T.J. & Jelissa**

A DOPEBOY'S PRAYER **II**

By **Eddie "Wolf" Lee**

IF LOVING YOU IS WRONG... **III**

By **Jelissa**

TRUE SAVAGE **VII**

MIDNIGHT CARTEL III

DOPE BOY MAGIC IV

By **Chris Green**

BLAST FOR ME **III**

A SAVAGE DOPEBOY III

CUTTHROAT MAFIA II

By **Ghost**

A HUSTLER'S DECEIT III

KILL ZONE **II**

BAE BELONGS TO ME III

A DOPE BOY'S QUEEN II

By **Aryanna**

CHAINED TO THE STREETS III

By **J-Blunt**

COKE KINGS V

KING OF THE TRAP II

By **T.J. Edwards**

GORILLAZ IN THE BAY V

TEARS OF A GANGSTA II

**De'Kari**

THE STREETS ARE CALLING II

**Duquie Wilson**

KINGPIN KILLAZ IV

STREET KINGS III

PAID IN BLOOD III

CARTEL KILLAZ IV

DOPE GODS II

**Hood Rich**

SINS OF A HUSTLA II

**ASAD**

TRIGGADALE III

**Elijah R. Freeman**

KINGZ OF THE GAME V

**Playa Ray**

SLAUGHTER GANG IV

RUTHLESS HEART IV

**By Willie Slaughter**

THE HEART OF A SAVAGE III

**By Jibril Williams**

FUK SHYT II

**By Blakk Diamond**

THE DOPEMAN'S BODYGAURD II

**By Tranay Adams**

TRAP GOD II

**By Troublesome**

YAYO III

A SHOOTER'S AMBITION III

**By S. Allen**

GHOST MOB

**Stilloan Robinson**

KINGPIN DREAMS II

**By Paper Boi Rari**

CREAM

**By Yolanda Moore**

SON OF A DOPE FIEND II

**By Renta**

FOREVER GANGSTA II

GLOCKS ON SATIN SHEETS II

**By Adrian Dulan**

LOYALTY AIN'T PROMISED II

**By Keith Williams**

THE PRICE YOU PAY FOR LOVE II

DOPE GIRL MAGIC III

**By Destiny Skai**

CONFESSIONS OF A GANGSTA II

**By Nicholas Lock**

I'M NOTHING WITHOUT HIS LOVE II

**By Monet Dragun**

CAUGHT UP IN THE LIFE III

**By Robert Baptiste**

NEW TO THE GAME III

By **Malik D. Rice**

LIFE OF A SAVAGE III

By **Romell Tukes**

QUIET MONEY II

By **Trai'Quan**

THE STREETS MADE ME II

By **Larry D. Wright**

THE ULTIMATE SACRIFICE VI

By **Anthony Fields**

THE LIFE OF A HOOD STAR

**By Ca$h & Rashia Wilson**

## Available Now

RESTRAINING ORDER **I & II**

By **CA$H & Coffee**

LOVE KNOWS NO BOUNDARIES **I II & III**

By **Coffee**

RAISED AS A GOON I, II,  III & IV

BRED BY THE SLUMS I, II, III

BLAST FOR ME I & II

ROTTEN TO THE CORE I II III

A BRONX TALE I, II, III

DUFFEL BAG CARTEL I II III IV

HEARTLESS GOON I II III IV

A SAVAGE DOPEBOY I II

HEARTLESS GOON I II III

DRUG LORDS I II III

CUTTHROAT MAFIA

By **Ghost**

LAY IT DOWN **I & II**

LAST OF A DYING BREED

BLOOD STAINS OF A SHOTTA I & II III

By **Jamaica**

LOYAL TO THE GAME I II III

LIFE OF SIN I, II III

By **TJ & Jelissa**

BLOODY COMMAS I & II

SKI MASK CARTEL I  II & III

KING OF NEW YORK I II,III IV V

RISE TO POWER I II III

COKE KINGS I II III IV

BORN HEARTLESS I II III IV

KING OF THE TRAP

By **T.J. Edwards**

IF LOVING HIM IS WRONG…I & II

LOVE ME EVEN WHEN IT HURTS I II III

By **Jelissa**

WHEN THE STREETS CLAP BACK I & II III

THE HEART OF A SAVAGE I II

By **Jibril Williams**

A DISTINGUISHED THUG STOLE MY HEART I II & III

LOVE SHOULDN'T HURT I II III IV

RENEGADE BOYS I II III IV

PAID IN KARMA I II III

By **Meesha**

A GANGSTER'S CODE I &, II III

A GANGSTER'S SYN I II III

THE SAVAGE LIFE I II III

CHAINED TO THE STREETS I II

**By J-Blunt**

PUSH IT TO THE LIMIT

By **Bre' Hayes**

BLOOD OF A BOSS **I, II, III, IV, V**

SHADOWS OF THE GAME

By **Askari**

THE STREETS BLEED MURDER **I, II & III**

THE HEART OF A GANGSTA I II& III

By **Jerry Jackson**

CUM FOR ME I II III IV V

An **LDP Erotica Collaboration**

BRIDE OF A HUSTLA **I  II & II**

THE FETTI GIRLS **I, II& III**

CORRUPTED BY A GANGSTA I, II III, IV

BLINDED BY HIS LOVE

THE PRICE YOU PAY FOR LOVE

DOPE GIRL MAGIC I II

By **Destiny Skai**

WHEN A GOOD GIRL GOES BAD

By **Adrienne**

THE COST OF LOYALTY I II III

**By Kweli**

A GANGSTER'S REVENGE **I II III & IV**

THE BOSS MAN'S DAUGHTERS I II III IV V

A SAVAGE LOVE **I & II**

BAE BELONGS TO ME I II

A HUSTLER'S DECEIT I, II, III

WHAT BAD BITCHES DO I, II, III

SOUL OF A MONSTER I II III

KILL ZONE

A DOPE BOY'S QUEEN

By **Aryanna**

A KINGPIN'S AMBITON

A KINGPIN'S AMBITION **II**

I MURDER FOR THE DOUGH

By **Ambitious**

TRUE SAVAGE I II III IV V VI

DOPE BOY MAGIC I, II, III

MIDNIGHT CARTEL I II

By **Chris Green**

A DOPEBOY'S PRAYER

By **Eddie "Wolf" Lee**

THE KING CARTEL **I, II & III**

By **Frank Gresham**

THESE NIGGAS AIN'T LOYAL **I, II & III**

By **Nikki Tee**

GANGSTA SHYT **I II &III**

By **CATO**

THE ULTIMATE BETRAYAL

By **Phoenix**

BOSS'N UP **I , II & III**

By **Royal Nicole**

I LOVE YOU TO DEATH

**By Destiny J**

I RIDE FOR MY HITTA

I STILL RIDE FOR MY HITTA

By **Misty Holt**

LOVE & CHASIN' PAPER

By **Qay Crockett**

TO DIE IN VAIN

SINS OF A HUSTLA

By **ASAD**

BROOKLYN HUSTLAZ

By **Boogsy Morina**

BROOKLYN ON LOCK I & II

By **Sonovia**

GANGSTA CITY

By **Teddy Duke**

A DRUG KING AND HIS DIAMOND I & II III

A DOPEMAN'S RICHES

HER MAN, MINE'S TOO I, II

CASH MONEY HO'S

**By Nicole Goosby**

TRAPHOUSE KING **I II & III**

KINGPIN KILLAZ I II III

STREET KINGS I II

PAID IN BLOOD **I II**

CARTEL KILLAZ I II III

DOPE GODS

By **Hood Rich**

LIPSTICK KILLAH **I, II, III**

CRIME OF PASSION I II & III

By **Mimi**

STEADY MOBBN' **I, II, III**

THE STREETS STAINED MY SOUL

By **Marcellus Allen**

WHO SHOT YA **I, II, III**

SON OF A DOPE FIEND

**Renta**

GORILLAZ IN THE BAY **I II III IV**

TEARS OF A GANGSTA

**DE'KARI**

TRIGGADALE I II

**Elijah R. Freeman**

GOD BLESS THE TRAPPERS I, II, III

THESE SCANDALOUS STREETS I, II, III

FEAR MY GANGSTA I, II, III

THESE STREETS DON'T LOVE NOBODY I, II

BURY ME A G I, II, III, IV, V

A GANGSTA'S EMPIRE I, II, III, IV

THE DOPEMAN'S BODYGAURD

**Tranay Adams**

THE STREETS ARE CALLING

**Duquie Wilson**

MARRIED TO A BOSS… I II III

**By Destiny Skai & Chris Green**

KINGZ OF THE GAME I  II III IV

**Playa Ray**

SLAUGHTER GANG I II III

RUTHLESS HEART I II III

**By Willie Slaughter**

FUK SHYT

**By Blakk Diamond**

DON'T F#CK WITH MY HEART I II

**By Linnea**

ADDICTED TO THE DRAMA I II III

**By Jamila**

YAYO I II

A SHOOTER'S AMBITION I II

**By S. Allen**

TRAP GOD

**By Troublesome**

FOREVER GANGSTA

GLOCKS ON SATIN SHEETS

**By Adrian Dulan**

TOE TAGZ I II III

**By Ah'Million**

KINGPIN DREAMS

**By Paper Boi Rari**

CONFESSIONS OF A GANGSTA

**By Nicholas Lock**

I'M NOTHING WITHOUT HIS LOVE

**By Monet Dragun**

CAUGHT UP IN THE LIFE I II

**By Robert Baptiste**

NEW TO THE GAME I II

By **Malik D. Rice**

Life of a Savage I II

By **Romell Tukes**

LOYALTY AIN'T PROMISED

**By Keith Williams**

Quiet Money

By **Trai'Quan**

THE STREETS MADE ME

By **Larry D. Wright**

THE ULTIMATE SACRIFICE I, II, III, IV, V

KHADIFI

By **Anthony Fields**

THE LIFE OF A HOOD STAR

**By Ca$h & Rashia Wilson**

## BOOKS BY LDP'S CEO, CA$H

TRUST IN NO MAN

TRUST IN NO MAN 2

TRUST IN NO MAN 3

BONDED BY BLOOD

SHORTY GOT A THUG

THUGS CRY

THUGS CRY 2

THUGS CRY 3

TRUST NO BITCH

TRUST NO BITCH 2

TRUST NO BITCH 3

TIL MY CASKET DROPS

RESTRAINING ORDER

RESTRAINING ORDER 2

IN LOVE WITH A CONVICT

LIFE OF A HOOD STAR

**Coming Soon**

BONDED BY BLOOD 2

BOW DOWN TO MY GANGSTA